·Dice Gods·

DICE GODS

HOPE HILL

Ink Drop Press
Chico, California

ISBN 13: 978-1-947583-19-1

Printed in the United States of America
Cover copyright by Ink Drop Press
*Cover design by **Zendesign** @ Bookcovers.com*

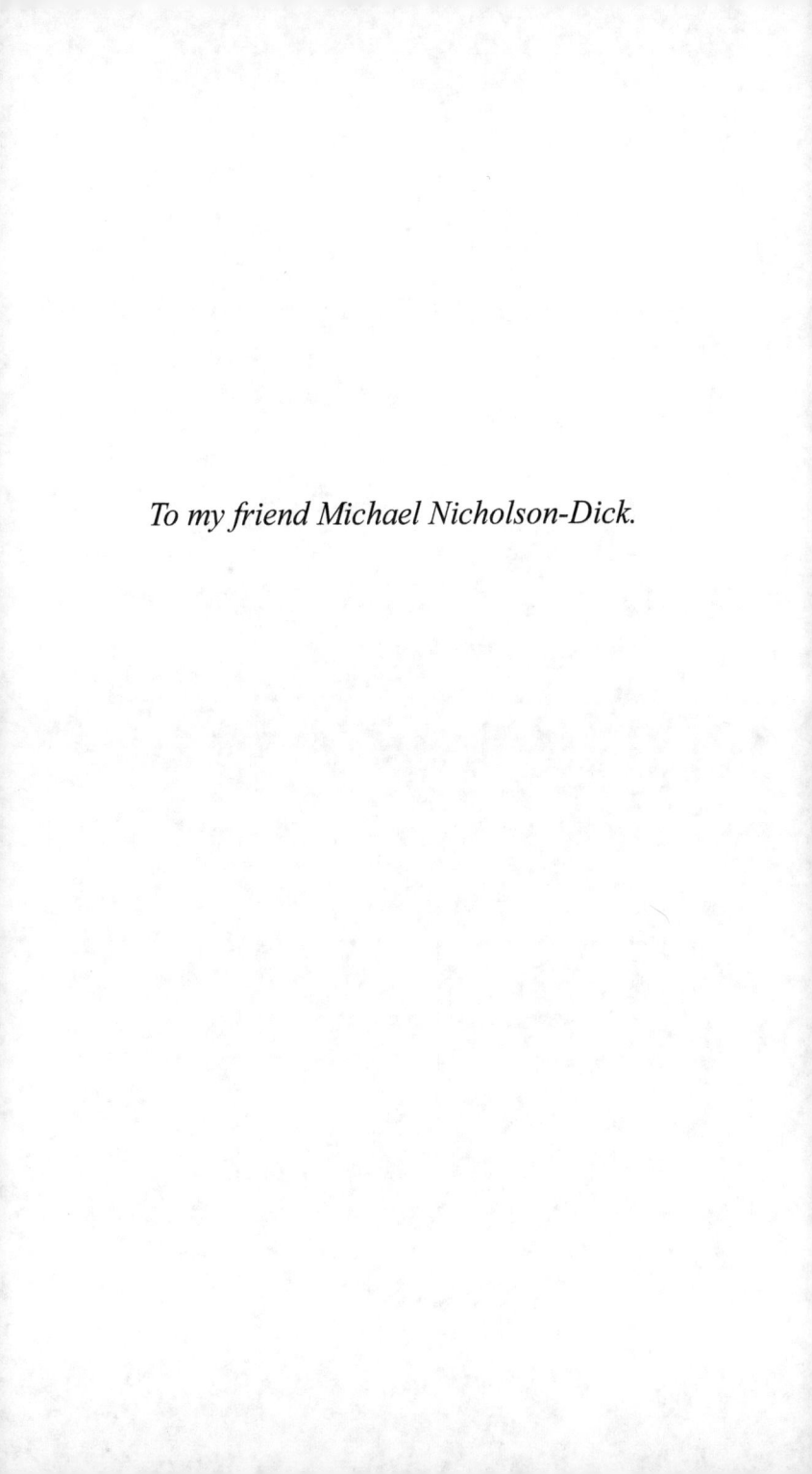

To my friend Michael Nicholson-Dick.

PROLOGUE

In a desolate valley, a four pointed star lay inside a circle and the air seemed to vibrate with anticipation. The ritual was about to begin. Four glowing beings were dragged towards each other. Each of the beings came from a different direction and they were pulled towards the four points of the star. The beings struggled to escape the ritual and avoid being placed inside the circle. None of them knew what was happening or why but they were sure that whatever it was they wanted no part in it.

A glowing man was pulled to the top of the star and when he reached it the circle lit up and his aura was sucked into the circle pulling the others closer. A corpse pale man in a dusty suit that seemed to get skinnier by the second wound up at the southern tip of the star. The zombie's deathly aura was pulled into the circle as well. A dusky skinned demon was pulled into the eastern point of the star and the Ifrit's powers were used to fuel the circle. Finally a fae with dragonfly wings was pulled into the western point of the star. The circle closed as it began to drain the Sylph of magic.

The four-pointed star inside the circle started to glow and drained all of their magic. The zombie fell first, the magic preventing them from breaking the circle when they passed out. The Sylph succumbed next, then the Ifrit lost consciousness. Finally the man with the glowing aura collapsed. The ritual continued and when it was finished the circle stopped glowing and the four of them collapsed, breaking the circle. None of them knew it, but their lives had just changed forever in ways none of them could've predicted.

Chapter 1
Waking Up

Dennis woke first. He looked around, clutching his head. He hadn't had a headache this bad since the drunken weekend that resulted in him achieving godhood. Whatever ritual he'd been part of left him feeling weak, dizzy and ravenous. He couldn't remember the last time he'd been this hungry. He usually fed off chaos and that was never in short supply.

When you live in a world where someone can become a god by getting drunk and challenging a stranger to games of chance; chaos is everywhere. Contrary to popular belief, he hadn't reached godhood by winning a game of poker. The winning poker hand granted him immortality but he'd taken the chaos god's divinity by winning a game of Jenga.

When Dennis won they both stared at each other for awhile before the hooded stranger explained the job. He still knew very little about his predecessor; just that they were a chaos deity instead of **the** Chaos Deity. Apparently there are levels of godhood and Dennis accidentally stumbled upon the lowest one.

The hunger grew until he could barely think. He closed his eyes and wished for some tasty chaos. When he opened them there was no food and the rumbling in his stomach was growing louder. The sound was blood curdling. He looked down at his stomach and immediately wished he hadn't. His clothes were filthy and his hands were emaciated. Whatever happened to him must have removed any nutrients he'd had, reducing him to this pitiful form.

He patted his pockets hoping to find food inside them. He hadn't remembered stashing food in them but he didn't remember putting on the black suit either. He was in luck. There was some bread stashed in his pocket. He ate it and the hunger subsided. It wasn't as nourishing as his normal fare, but it was all he had.

Now that he could think again he looked around. He remembered hurtling towards a four pointed star inside a ritual circle with arcane markings. He vaguely recalled being used to power the ritual and seeing others pulled into the circle as well. He searched for them and saw three sleeping figures. They must still be unconscious after the effects of the ritual. Since he'd had the most power stolen he should've woken last not first.

Still as a chaos god, plans tended to go awry around him. He must've made the magic go wonky. Hopefully he wasn't too far from home. He'd need a decent source of chaos to be able to find out what had been done and if he should reverse it. Although given how lousy he felt he wasn't certain he'd care once he found out why he'd been subjected to a ritual and had his power sucked out like someone shotgunning a beer. He didn't like being the beer.

With that in mind he began to plan his revenge. He would find whoever or whatever was responsible and make them pay. He'd show everyone why it's considered a bad idea to anger a god; especially a god of Chaos.

Perhaps he'd ask the others for their input before deciding on a final punishment. When he knew all of the crimes against him he would wreak his vengeance. It would be devastating but fair. As a god of Chaos he knew enough other gods and goddesses who owed him favors to ensure that even if those responsible for this atrocity died before being punished they would not escape his wrath.

His plotting was interrupted when one of the shapes began moving. "Ow. My head." A musical voice proclaimed before shrieking. "What happened to me?"

The being screamed. "You will suffer for the insult done to Izal Sunbound. I will find the one who stuffed me in this....form and they will pay." The one screaming ,slightly shorter than Dennis with long sky colored hair and enormous dragonfly wings.

"Izal Sunbound is a weird name for a Sylph." Dennis said as he laughed at the being's rage.

"That is because I am not a Sylph. I am an Ifrit. A powerful demon and being trapped in such a pathetic body is a greater insult than I can bear. Besides, I don't think a Zombie has any room to criticize." Izal retorted.

"I am not a Zombie." Dennis said, wishing to smite the irritating Sylph.

"What are you, some kind of Unlife Activist? Would you prefer to be called Reanimated or Undead?" Izal mocked.

"Actually I'm Dennis Murphy, a Chaos god. You can call me Dennis or Murphy or Chaos god." Dennis replied.

"What kind of chaos god is named Dennis

Murphy?" Izal asked.

"I used to be mortal. It's not like my parents knew I'd become a chaos god. Besides, chaos gods are part of the reason Murphy's law exists." Dennis said with a smirk.

"Oh, really and what's the other part?" Izal asked, lifting one perfectly arched brow.

"Magic, morons, and malice." Dennis said with a shrug.

"That still doesn't explain why a Zombie is talking to me claiming to be a chaos god of all things." Izal insisted.

Dennis looked down noticing his grey skin and skeletal appearance.. His expression darkened and for a moment Izal could understand how a Zombie could claim to be a god. "I thought they'd merely stolen my power to fuel a ritual or two. If I'm stuck in this form then you probably are an Ifrit trapped in a Sylph's body which means that one of us has a Sylph running around in our body and the other has a Zombie shuffling along in theirs." Dennis said, hands clenched in rage.

"On second thought, being stuck in this body is less irritating than being trapped as a Zombie. I think I'd rather have a Sylph in my body than a Zombie." Izal admitted.

"I don't blame you. But until the others wake up we won't know. I think the weakest forms are waking first. Which means Zombie, then Sylph, then Ifrit, then chaos god." Dennis explained.

"So it's based on how much power the body has, not how much power the spirit has." Izal said.

"That's the only explanation for why I woke up first. I'm powerful so if it was based on spirit then I'd have woken up last. I suspect that all of our powers are diminished and can only be accessed by the person in the body they belong to. Otherwise I'd have turned you into a toad for your insults." Dennis said glaring at Izal.

"True. I am more powerful than a Sylph and your insults should have resulted in me trying to burn you alive but I couldn't make a spark. Upside is this ritual proves that some powers at least are anchored to the body. If I can provide evidence of this I might even be able to make enough money to buy an office and start up collateral to make an Ifrit Consulting Firm," Izal said with a demonic smile.

"Perhaps you should leave the dreaming of what to do with your vast amount of loot 'til after we've found out who did this to us and gotten revenge," Dennis said.

"That's fair. After all, we do need to repay this egregious insult," Izal agreed.

With those words another shape began to stir. "Did I overindulge in elven wine again?" A booming voice asked. The loud sound startled the creature who looked down seeing a dusky-skinned demon and the telltale feel of transformation magic. "Aaaaaaaaa! What happened to my beautiful body? Why have I been turned into some hideous beast? Waaaaaaaaahhhhhh!" The voice asked.

Dennis buried his head in his hands and sobbed.

"Oi. That is my body and I'll thank you not to disparage it. I'm a very attractive Ifrit; besides, what am I supposed to do with this fragile Sylph body," Izal insisted.

Dennis sobbed louder.

"Oh, I didn't realize this was your body. I thought I got changed into a creature again and was hoping that crying and looking miserable would result in a quicker return to normal," the being said, as if the previous wailing was perfectly understandable.

"Does getting turned into something else happen to you a lot?" Izal asked as Dennis continued to sob in the background.

"Only when my relatives are mad at me or parties get out of hand. Usually it's a result of someone being mad at someone else or overindulging in elven wine. Other than that, not really. Maybe three or four times a year," the being explained.

Dennis sobbed even louder.

"What's his problem?" The being asked.

"He's a chaos god and they stuffed him into a Zombie body. He's crying because that means the Zombie is stuck in his body. He was hoping you were in his body instead." Izal explained.

"I suppose I would cry too if I was swapped with a Zombie." The being said before walking over to pat Dennis on the head. "There, there. I'm Arith. I got stuck as a swamp monster for a week once. There was a party and my cousin said I looked fat. I got mad so I told my cousin that at least I wasn't the one lying on my college applications pretending to be a nymph. Unfortunately nobody heard what my cousin said but everyone heard my response. My cousin lost their scholarship. Rather than getting mad at my cousin for lying about their species to get into a better school they got mad at me for outing my cousin." Arith explained.

"Not that that wasn't an interesting story, but was there a point to it?" Dennis asked once they'd stopped crying.

"You feel better don't you?" Arith asked.

"Well, yes." Dennis admitted.

"Then the story helped." Arith said.

"How do you know your cousin was lying about being a nymph? I thought Sylphs and Nymphs were basically the same." Izal said

"Sylphs are air elementals. Nymphs are Sprites, usually water sprites but there's also other types of sprites. Elementals and Sprites are as different as brownies and leprechauns. My cousin lied because Nymphs don't usually go to university since they are typically bound to a place. So my cousin claimed to be a nymph to get a scholarship since there wouldn't be much competition. Sylphs are generally nomadic so we don't go to universities often either. If my cousin had told the truth they'd probably have gotten a scholarship and they wouldn't have had to worry about getting caught." Arith explained, shaking their head.

"Wait, your cousin lied to get a spot they could've gotten by telling the truth and then when they got caught you were blamed?" Izal asked.

"Pretty much." Arith said.

"That's messed up." Dennis added. "When I'm back to being a chaos god do you want me to give your cousin a visit?"

"I'd settle for them receiving the information proving that the truth would've been more helpful than a lie and an apology for turning me into a swamp monster." Arith admitted.

"Well, you're certainly nicer than I'd be under the circumstances." Dennis admitted while Izal nodded.

"Your cousin deserves far worse. Lying would be bad enough but throwing someone else into the line of fire to save yourself is deplorable. If your cousin is willing to use those kinds of tactics to get their way then they don't deserve your protection. You don't have to deal with them still do you?" Izal asked.

"No. I left home after that. I'd been thinking about leaving before that but afterwards knowing that no-one defended me convinced me. I know they probably forgave me but I don't think what I did was unforgivable. Especially since I'm not the one who told the college admissions board. I didn't even know which schools my cousin applied to. I only found out since they were bragging about scamming the system. I got the blame and nobody bothered to find out the truth. I haven't been back since." Arith paused.

"Does anyone ever ask how you're doing?" Izal asked.

"My parents and siblings send me letters occasionally telling me they miss me. Still all of them think I lied about what happened and that it's my fault my cousin's applications got rejected. The worst part is knowing that they don't trust me." Arith said, hanging their head.

"I'm sorry. Do you think it would help if you moved back and tried to explain it now that time has passed?" Izal asked.

"I moved out so I could put down roots. I wanted to live somewhere where people would know me well enough to believe me. Ironically my cousin was the reason I went to college. I ended up going to a university and staying until I got my bachelor's degree. I didn't switch schools or lie on the application. I just did the work. That's another reason I think my cousin's an idiot. The truth is the reason I got a scholarship and was able to put myself through school." Arith said, eyes glinting at the thought of the revenge none of their family knew they'd gotten.

"Any chance you want a copy of your school records and application to be included in the mountain of evidence that will mysteriously find its way to every member of your family?" Dennis asked with a vicious smirk.

"I'd like that. Mostly because I want the luxury of telling them off when they finally admit that they were wrong and offer to let me come home."

Chapter 2
What Happened?

Just as Arith's smirk started to fade the final figure began to stir. The figure stretched. "My head is pounding. Why does my voice sound weird." The being looked down to see a body that was was perfectly sculpted with details that seemed to shift when he wasn't looking and glowed with power. "AAAAAAAAAHHHHHHHH! Why am I glowing? What happened to me?"

"What happened is that someone or something decided it would be fun to do a ritual that swapped our bodies. Surely you remember the force pulling you towards the ritual circle before you collapsed." Dennis said.

"That doesn't explain why I'm glowing!" The being screeched.

"You're glowing because you wound up in my body and I'm a chaos god. The glow is caused by my aura. Normally I'd turn it off if I wanted to go incognito but since I can't control my powers right now you'll have to do it," Dennis admitted.

"I don't know how. I've never glowed before. How am I supposed to know how to stop glowing?" The being questioned.

"Do you want to be glowing?" Dennis asked.

"Well, no."

"Then think about that and the glowing will stop," Dennis instructed.

"It's not working."

"Do you believe you can make the glowing stop?" Dennis asked.

"No."

"Magic is simple. It takes four things. One: a desire for something. Two: a belief that the thing can happen. Three: the power to make it happen. Four: the control required to make it happen. When you know more about magic you can accomplish it with a thought but for now you'll need to focus on all four components." Dennis explained.

"Isn't there any other advice you could give me?" The being asked.

"None that you'd understand. Besides, this is how I was taught to use my powers which means it's how you'll be taught to use my powers. There are other ways to learn magic but we're going to stick with learning how to control my powers before you start accidentally turning people into toads."

"So, it's fine if I turn people into toads on purpose?" The being questioned.

"You're in the body of a c haos god, so yes. However if you turn me into a toad or any other kind of creature I will retaliate and since I'm currently in your body my revenge would be swift and sweet," Dennis smirked.

"Alright then. Before Dennis gives you any more advice I think I should point out that since it took all four of us to power up the initial ritual it will probably take all four of us to reverse it," Izal added, not feeling like being turned into a random creature.

"That's true and I will do my best to keep from turning anyone here into a random creature. After the events of today I think we can all agree that we've been through enough changes already," The being agreed.

"I'm Arith and I'm a Sylph but I'm in Izal's body. Izal is a delightful Ifrit although I do wish we met under better circumstances. You already know that Dennis is the chaos god you got your body swapped with. You know all of our names but none of us know yours. Would you mind telling us?" Arith asked.

If anyone had looked they would've noticed Izal

blushing but they were all busy doing other things. Even Izal didn't notice the blush; they'd never done so before and were unfamiliar with the feeling.

"Oh, I'm Gregory Savage but you can call me Greg. I'm an Unlife Activist so I prefer the term Undead. As you can tell I can think and talk just fine, even when I'm not trapped in a chaos god's body. I'm not a cannibal and despite being undead for the past six years I've never experienced any problems with my flesh disintegrating or falling to pieces. So if you don't mind I'd rather not be called a 'Zombie'," Greg explained.

"Okay. That does seem to indicate that you aren't a Zombie. Do you drink blood?" Arith asked.

"No. I probably could but I don't," Greg said with a smile.

"You could drink blood but you don't. What is that supposed to mean?" Izal asked.

"Exactly what I said. I probably could drink blood. I just have no desire to. Besides, any of us could drink blood. It doesn't kill you. Plenty of people like their meat bloody and others stick their fingers in their mouths when they have a paper cut. It's only considered taboo if you engage in cannibalism, drink someone's blood without permission or kill them to get said blood," Greg said as if this was perfectly reasonable.

"Am I the only one getting creeped out here?" Dennis asked.

"No," Izal and Arith answered in unison.

"I don't see what the problem is. I got asked a question and I answered it," Greg said.

"I may have asked but I was not expecting that response. I regretted asking the minute you answered," Izal replied.

"If you didn't want to know the answer, then why did you ask the question?" Greg asked.

"I was trying to determine what species you are," Izal admitted.

"I'm undead. I woke up in my coffin and couldn't

remember anything other than my first name. I knew that I was Gregory. Savage is the last name my boss gave me. The application wouldn't go through unless I had a last name. Never mind that I'd only been undead for three days so I was technically a newborn. Apparently Savage is a popular last name for the undead. I did have to sit through a video about why biting the customers is grounds for termination of employment but I did like working at the pub," Greg said.

"You got hired to work at a bar. Doesn't that violate some kind of health code?" Izal asked.

"Only if I tracked grave dirt everywhere or dropped pieces of myself. Since I'm not decomposing and I don't carry any diseases there's nothing that prevents me from working there. Besides, I'm not the only member of the Undead who works at The Defiant Badger Pub," Greg taunted.

"No. We're not discussing this any further. Greg's employment is none of our business. We need to figure out how to undo this and let whoever did this know just why it's a terrible idea to piss off a bunch of powerful people. Greg, it's time for you to stop glowing. It's distracting. It hurts my eyes and it makes you an easy target for an ambush." Dennis said while he waited for his demands to be met.

"Alright, what do we know about this ritual?" Izal asked.

"It's a ritual using a four-pointed star. We were each summoned from a different direction. All of us had energy stolen to fuel the ritual and we all ended up body swapped. The amount of energy stolen is more than it would take to swap all of us. Which means that our energy is out there somewhere either being contained or used as a battery source. I for one don't like the idea of letting whoever did this to me succeed with whatever they're planning." Dennis insisted.

"Fair enough. I'm not familiar enough with rituals that include four-pointed stars to figure out why the star included four points instead of the traditional five,"

Izal admitted.

"Four is an even number but it has some less than stellar implications. It's often associated with death, which might be why there are two ways to split the elements. Water, Fire, Earth, and Air or Water, Fire, Earth, Air and Spirit/Magic." Arith explained.

"Huh. I always thought the fifth element was Chaos," Dennis added.

"Someone's a bit full of themself." Greg teased.

"I didn't ask for your opinion," Dennis griped.

"Fellas. Calm down. We need to work together to figure this out," Izal insisted.

"I think it'll be fine. We just need to determine why they chose us and the significance of the ritual so we can craft a counter ritual," Arith added, smiling.

"Or we could just find whoever's involved and torture them until they agree to fix it before unleashing our vengeance," Izal suggested.

Arith glared at Izal. "Really?"

"Hey, I'm an Ifrit," Izal said. "Just because I'm in

your body doesn't make me less of a demon. Besides, you can't deny that you want vengeance. You're an elemental and nature is not known to be forgiving."

"Can we get back to the task at hand. Whoever did this planned it meticulously. They made certain I would reach the circle first and take the first point in the star. I was placed in the northern point, Greg was placed in the southern point, Izal was placed in the Eastern point and Arith was placed in the western point. Ifrits are associated with fire and Sylphs are Air Elementals. I suppose Zombies could fill in for Earth but chaos gods are not associated with water. If there'd been five points I could've been the counterpart for spirit or magic. This means the four points aren't supposed to reference the four elements or if they are it's not a combination of elements we'd recognize," Dennis admitted.

"Huh. I didn't think of that. Do you think you could find someone to help us? We need a direction to go in. I'm not sure where we are and it's not like there's a convenient magic trail to follow," Arith said with a sigh.

"If I still had access to my magic I might have been able to fix that. As it stands though, I've got nothing. Now as much as I like how this conversation is going, I'm starving and I don't know what's safe for this body to eat." Dennis said as his stomach let out a horrifying growl.

"I'm vegetarian. I won't eat anything that can talk to me. Other than that I don't have any dietary restrictions. Before my first paycheck arrived I ate anything that was available and lacking sentience. I ate trash for three weeks. Beer bottles aren't bad," Greg admitted.

"That's disturbing but I suppose it's good to know. I think I'd rather have real food though. I'm fairly certain you shouldn't be eating glass bottles," Dennis said as he started scouting around in search of food items.

"Alright. If you're going to be picky about it I

should have some coins in my pocket that'll cover a meal but make sure someone else orders for you. I don't want to get a reputation as a thief because you ate more food than you paid for," Greg insisted.

"Well, I never, in all my years, expected to deal with that level of insult. I was going to be nice but if you're going to be rude then I'm going to order a rare steak to see if they'll serve it to me raw," Dennis threatened.

"I thought we agreed to stop fighting and focus on the task at hand." Arith asked.

"The task at hand is that he's being rude and if I'm not given food soon I'm going to start eating whatever's closest and most annoying," Dennis muttered.

"You can't eat Greg. You don't know what it would do to you and he's currently in your body. Do you want to be a Zombie for eternity or worse because I'm fairly certain eating a god while it's still alive is a very bad idea." Izal said, shuddering at the idea of the unholy abomination that could create.

"Alright, I won't eat him. Now can we please get me some food. I wasn't kidding about being ravenously hungry. I'm pretty sure I could cheerfully eat a trashcan right now if it would stop the hunger pangs," Dennis whined.

"That's disturbing," Izal muttered. "We'll get you food but you need to stop fighting with Greg while we figure out what direction food is in."

"Fine. I'll stop fighting with him for now but if he doesn't stop insulting me I'm smiting him as soon as I get my body back," Dennis promised.

"That's fair, just try and hold on until then. I'll talk with him and see if I can convince him to back off," Izal suggested trying to keep the peace.

Izal walked over to Greg. "You know that if you don't knock it off he'll kill you as soon as he's back in his rightful body don't you?"

"Just because he's a god doesn't mean he has the right to treat people however he wants," Greg insisted.

"No. Being a god doesn't give him that power. People deciding they'd rather obey than get smote gives him that power," Izal said, trying not to lose their patience.

"I'm undead. I'm not sure how scared I should be of dying," Greg retorted.

"Do you honestly think a little thing like potential immortality will prevent him from getting revenge for real or imagined slights. He's a god. He'll either rewrite the laws of physics or torture you for eternity. Do you really want to find out if the sun explodes before his anger dissipates?" Izal asked.

"When you say it like that it sounds bad," Greg admitted his cockiness vanished once he understood the reality of the situation. Izal glared at him. "I promise to stop picking fights with him."

Chapter 3
We Need to Work Together

Now that the initial arguing was over, Arith spoke. "Fighting hasn't gotten us anywhere so until someone has something useful to discuss I want everyone to zip it."

"Who made you the leader?" Dennis asked.

"You did when your inability to get along with people started causing problems." Arith replied.

"Greg started it."

"I don't care who started it. I ended it. You can worry about getting revenge later. For now, it might help to remember that he currently has your body and your powers. So if you don't want to be turned into a snake, I'd stop being obnoxious. Besides, I don't think you want sandstorms to follow you around for the next twenty years." Arith threatened.

"You don't have your powers either." Dennis retorted.

"No but my current form is that of an Ifrit. Do you really want to see what I'm capable of in this form? Besides, if you continue to be obnoxious you might anger Izal as well and since we already get along I think we could work together to use our powers against you." Arith said with a terrifying smile.

"Is that supposed to scare me?" Dennis asked.

"Not necessarily, but it should help you think before you speak." Arith replied.

"Arith's the only one who hasn't pissed me off and if combining forces with a Sylph gets you two to stop arguing and all of us back into our proper bodies, I'll do so." Izal said with a devious smirk.

"Aw. That's sweet. I'd be delighted to team up with you and help sort out these arrogant pricks. Who knows, you might decide to visit me at my home? I'm certain my nosy neighbors would be shocked. They're always telling me I need to get out more and meet new people and I think it would end the blatant attempts at matchmaking." Arith said with a grin.

"It'll be much funnier if you tell them we met in costume." Izal suggested.

"This is why I think it'd be nice to introduce you to my neighbors. The terrible blind dates would stop and I'd get to laugh at a bunch of inside jokes. I can see it now. 'I've never had anyone else understand me like Izal does.' The only problem would be keeping from laughing as I said it." Arith smiled.

"Am I the only one who isn't sure how to solve this?" Greg asked.

"No. The first step is figuring out where we are so we can work on determining what direction to go in." Arith suggested.

Izal looked around at the desolate landscape. "I think I might know where we are."

"Really, where?" Everyone else asked in unison.

"I think we're in the Underworld. If I'm right, we're on the outskirts of the Underworld. There are better places to perform a ritual down here but none of the other spots are isolated enough to pull off this kind of ritual without getting caught." Izal explained.

"Why the Underworld?" Dennis scoffed.

"Maybe they thought the person with the most power here would be Greg and he can't use it in Dennis' body." Izal said.

"Does that mean someone else has power here?" Dennis asked.

Izal smirked. "Yes. The Underworld isn't just the Realm of the Dead. It's also home to a Hell Dimension. Which is good for us and bad for whoever did this ritual."

"Why is it good for us?" Dennis asked.

"Because Hell Dimensions are home to Demons

and Ifrits are a type of Demon. Sylph's can use their powers anywhere there's air. The presence of Demons also increases the odds of chaos so if Dennis and Greg can work together we can harness some of that chaos and use it to our advantage." Izal replied.

"I like the way you think." Dennis said, thinking of all the ways they could get their revenge.

"Arith, what direction feels best to you?" Izal asked.

"Straight. I think I see a settlement up ahead."

"Greg, do you remember where the bar you work at is located?" Izal asked.

"It was a couple of blocks from the cemetery I woke up in."

"Okay. Do you remember what dimension that was in?" Izal asked.

"I don't know. I woke up wearing a suit in a wooden coffin, so I'm going to guess the Human Realm." Greg replied.

"Okay, so the bar is in the Human Realm. That's

good. The Underworld has a few different connections to the Human Realm. Since it doubles as the Realm of the Dead it has at least one connection to each realm. As a member of the Undead Greg should be able to leave at will. Dennis is a chaos god so he can do as he pleases. Ifrits are a Demonic race so I can leave at will and Sylphs are Air Elementals and no realm can contain an Elemental. This means escaping is not only plausible but probable." Izal answered.

"Well, I'm glad one of us is confident." Arith replied, smiling at Izal.

"Now the real question is what step we take from here. We could continue to explore the Underworld trying to find out who's responsible for swapping us and why they chose to do so. We could try to find someone capable of undoing this. We could try to leave this place and get as far from the ritual site as possible. We could try to master some of our temporary powers so that we aren't completely helpless or we could sit here and hope someone arrives to rescue us." Izal suggested.

"I don't like that last option. What if whoever arrives finds us helpless and takes advantage?" Dennis asked.

"Just because you're selfish and only view other people in terms of what they can do for you doesn't mean everyone feels that way." Greg chided.

"Guys, we've been over this. You need to chill out and quit fighting. We're not going to get anywhere if we keep bickering. We're not staying here but that doesn't mean the people we encounter will hurt us. We need to leave this spot because staying in a ritual circle increases the odds we'll end up involved in another ritual which will make it harder for us to return to our original bodies." Arith explained.

"Since nobody knows we were kidnapped nobody's looking for us which means staying put isn't going to help." Arith paused to catch a breath.

"If I have to warn you again I will be enlisting Izal's help in making both of you regret it. Keep in mind that Sylphs are also a type of Fae. I've warned you twice about what I'll do if you don't stop. Magic herself will force me to keep my word if I have to talk to you about this again." Arith threatened.

"Understood." Dennis and Greg said in unison.

"For the record, I'm not one of the Fae. I won't be teaching you a lesson because Magic commands it. I'll be doing it because you're pissing me off and I'm tired of it. Now hopefully everyone can agree to act like an adult from here on out," Izal said in a menacing tone nobody expected to come out of a Sylph's mouth.

Chapter 4
Knock it off, Guys

On that note, Dennis and Greg privately agreed that Izal and Arith were surprisingly intimidating. "Is there anything in particular you think we should do?" Greg asked.

"We should leave and try to master our powers," Dennis said, shuddering at the thought of what the Ifrit Sylph duo would do to him.

"We're headed towards the settlement Arith saw earlier. Greg; you and Dennis will need to work together to figure out your powers. Arith and I will

45

follow while working on ours. When we've made sufficient progress the two with the most control will end up leading and guarding our backs with the other two in the middle." Izal declared.

"You're just saying that because you think you're better than us." Dennis sneered.

Izal's eyes narrowed and the Sylph's body growled. "If you really want to prove that you're better than me, start showing some self control. Besides, part of why we're going to a settlement is because you need to eat something. Everyone else would be perfectly fine going without food while we're in unfamiliar territory." Izal scolded.

"How dare you treat me like a child. I'm a god and I demand to be treated like one." Dennis whined.

"If you act like a child I'll treat you like a child. If you want to be treated with respect you can earn it. Now move." Izal yelled, creating a small tornado that moved towards Dennis with frightening speed.

Dennis let out a yelp and hurried to follow orders.

Greg made another mental note to avoid angering Izal.

"Izal, you've just created your first tornado. I'm so proud of you." Arith proclaimed before pulling them into an embrace. "I remember the first time I created a tornado. Once you can use your powers intentionally and dismiss tornadoes as easily as you create them, you'll be considered an adult Sylph. You would make a fantastic suitor. Learning to harness the Air within hours of winding up in a Sylph body. You're a natural." Arith said, unaware of Izal's blush.

"Wouldn't your family be unhappy about you dating outside your species? I'm an Ifrit, not a Sylph." Izal said, seeming confused.

"Not really. I'm Fae. We don't worry as much about things like that. Besides, have you ever tried to summon a tornado before?" Arith asked.

"Well, no." Izal admitted.

"Then how do you know you couldn't as an Ifrit?" Arith asked.

"I guess I don't. There's still more to dating than

whether or not you share powers." Izal insisted.

"I know, but I have no intention of dating anyone. If I enter a relationship it will either be a tryst or courtship. It's either fleeting pleasure with no strings attached or a relationship that will hopefully end in a lifelong bond." Arith replied.

"So you won't date me but you think I'd make a good lifemate?" Izal asked, blushing so hard steam surrounded them.

This time everyone stared at Izal. Dennis and Greg decided not to say anything for fear of being attacked. "Yes. You're under no obligation to do anything about it. Besides, I said you would make a good suitor not that you will. There are other things I would need from a suitor before I could agree to courting but everything I've seen from you so far indicates you'd be worth courting." Arith said, smiling at Izal.

"Aren't you concerned I might not be single?" Izal asked.

"That will only matter if we attempt a courtship.

Right now all I know is that you're strong-willed, cunning, powerful, capable of compassion, and cruelty, your voice is sexy and we work well together. That's enough to consider you a potential suitor." Arith insisted.

"Good to know." Izal said, trying to control the steaming blush.

"Could we get back to trying to figure out what happened to us and how to fix it?" Dennis snarked.

"Oh, so when you're throwing a tantrum or fighting with Greg it's important but when Izal and I are discussing our potential courtship it's a waste of time. Rude much?" Arith complained before bursting into flames.

"That was rather intelligent. Piss off a Sylph in an Ifrit body. Fae reaction to insult paired with Demonic rage and a tendency to set things on Fire. Just brilliant. If you don't mind I'm going to watch Arith obliterate you. It'll be a fantastic courting gift." Izal admitted.

Abruptly the flames subsided. "Does that mean

you'll accept my courtship?" Arith asked.

"It means I'm willing to consider a courtship but in order to do it right, we'll need a long courtship. There are a lot of things we'll need to work out if we're going to be lifemates. Besides, I'd rather the bulk of our courtship not be observed by these two idiots. Once we reach the settlement we'll see about getting our courtship legally recognized and start the process. There will be no courting until then. We'll work out the rest later." Izal insisted.

Chapter 5
Heading to Civilization

The walk to the settlement was long and silent. Izal guarded the rear and Arith led the way. The two of them thought of what would happen when they reached the settlement. Dennis and Greg were just trying to avoid being attacked.

They reached the settlement as a group. "You two will need to go with us to register our courtship." Izal insisted.

"Why?" Dennis asked.

"Because you heard us discuss our intent to court

and the two of you are the only witnesses to us waking up body swapped. They'll need that information to document the situation properly. Besides, if we don't swap back soon we'll be stuck with you two as chaperones." Izal explained.

"What if we refuse?" Dennis asked.

"We'll see what happens to an immortal being once they've been attacked by a flaming tornado." Izal retorted.

"I don't want that. So where are we going and what do you need me to say?" Greg asked.

"Well, Dennis, should we perform an experiment or will you cooperate?" Izal asked.

"Alright, I'll do it. But when I'm a god again I'm going to get my revenge."

"You do that. Just remember, I'm a Demon and Arith's Fae. Neither species is known to handle threats or insults well." Izal replied.

"If we're all done threatening each other I'd like to register this courtship soon. I can't even hold Izal's hand until our courtship is legally recognized." Arith complained.

"Why not?" Greg asked, curiosity getting the best of him.

"Because Izal declared Intent. If Izal hadn't done so and insisted on a formal courtship then we wouldn't be bound to follow strict rules. Informal courtships take whatever form the courting couple wish but still tend to end in formal bonding. Formal courtships take longer and only end with the dissolution of the relationship or formal bonding. If a child is created during the courtship it will either end the relationship or result in formal bonding depending on who the child's parents are and how said child was created." Arith explained.

"Huh?" Greg asked.

"Cheating during a formal courtship will dissolve the relationship but if the child was created in a way that doesn't break the rules of the courtship then the courtship will immediately result in a formal bonding."Arith said, trying to explain it in simpler terms.

"Oh. That makes sense. So there must be ways that a child can be created that result in said child having parents that aren't involved in the courtship without breaking said courtship." Greg said.

"Yes. Sometimes there are more than two people involved and the child has fewer biological parents than members of the courtship but if both parents are courting even if the courtship has multiple members then it's fine. Things can get super complicated. Which is why many formal courtships limit the number of participants or limit what can be done before formally bonding." Arith added.

"I see." Greg blushed.

Chapter 6
Reaching the Temple

They arrived at a Demonic Temple and the group walked in unsure of their reception. They immediately saw a disheveled looking creature wearing long black robes covered in arcane symbols. "Greetings travelers, how may this humble servant help you?"

"You can start by ditching the spiel. We have a specific demand and you will either fulfill our demands or send us in the direction of someone who can." Izal insisted.

"Don't bother lying. We've got an Ifrit, a Sylph and a chaos god in our group so the only one you could really fool would be our undead member and he works in a bar." Arith said in the booming voice they'd become accustomed to.

"Alright then. Why don't you tell me what you need and I'll let you know if I can help," the being said now in plain black robes. They looked more indistinct but less disheveled letting them know a glamour was in place. Probably a layered one since the markings and pitiful vibe had both vanished but the creature could still not be identified.

"We need to register a formal courtship." Izal insisted.

"Between the four of you? Why would you bother to do so in the Underworld?" The robed being asked.

"No. Arith and I want to register a formal courtship." Izal said, pointing to Arith who waved. "We discussed courting and I declared my Intent to begin a Formal Courtship. Dennis and Greg witnessed our discussion. This was the nearest Temple and we had to do so in the Underworld since we met after a ritual summoned us here, drained some of our magic and swapped our bodies. Arith is a Sylph but stuck in my body. Greg is Undead but he's stuck in a chaos god's body. Dennis is a chaos god but he's stuck in an undead body. I'm Izal and I'm an Ifrit but I'm stuck in Arith's body."

"Okay. So you got body swapped in some weird ritual and you decided to begin a Formal Courtship with the person whose body you're stuck in?" The being asked. "And I thought my life was weird."

"Will you help us or not? I want to begin my courtship with Izal." Arith said as if that was all the information anyone needed.

"Alright. It isn't actually too difficult to do so. The hardest part will be ensuring it's your minds that are bound rather than your bodies. So I'm not going to do that. Instead we'll bind your essence to the courtship. It will make it harder to break the courtship but not impossible." The being assured them.

"If I find out this is some kind of trick to steal our souls you'll regret it." Izal threatened.

"Don't worry about it. Demon souls aren't all that useful and the Fae do not appreciate being stolen from and I'm not about to piss off the North Wind." The being muttered.

"Why would doing that piss off the North Wind?" Izal asked.

"Probably because he's my grandfather." Arith said.

"When were you going to tell me that?" Izal asked.

"Later. No point in scaring you off before knowing if you'll meet him." Arith explained.

"What if he hates me for courting you?" Izal asked.

"He wouldn't. He knows I'm an adult and I make my own choices." Arith said.

"What if we break up? Am I going to have to worry about him hunting me down?" Izal asked.

"No. I won't introduce you to him unless we have a child or decide to formally bond. In which case he'll love you for gifting me with a child and making me happy." Arith added.

"How do you know we'll even be able to have kids?" Izal asked.

"I'm Fae. If I want a child I'll have one." Arith insisted.

"You do know that it takes a man and a woman to make a baby right?" Dennis asked.

"Not if you're Fae. There are multiple ways to have a child. We could conceive a child naturally, or be blessed with a child, we could adopt a Changeling, I could make a child and that's just counting the most common ways for a Fae to wind up with a child." Arith explained.

"That explains a few things. I still have a few questions but they aren't important right now." Izal added.

"You're fine with this? You're not even going to ask what Arith is?" Dennis asked.

"Demons have too many shape shifting species to

care about things like that. Arith will inform me of any pertinent details when I need to know them. Stop asking me inappropriate questions about my future bondmate before Arith hears you. Unless you want to be attacked by a flaming tornado and have Arith's grandfather attack you." Izal threatened.

"Alright. I get it. You want me to shut up or face terrible consequences but did you really have to threaten me with the North Wind?" Dennis whined.

"Yes." Izal insisted.

Chapter 7
Formal Courtship

"If you two are done bickering I'm ready to begin." The robed being said, gesturing for everyone to come closer. "First of all, it's an honor to be able to record your courtship. I'm sure it'll be one for the record books. Tales will be told of your love."

"I told you to stop the tourist spiel." Izal growled.

"Just because you don't like what I'm saying doesn't mean I'm trying to sell you a line. Tales will be told of your love because Sylphs and Ifrits don't usually court each other. It's going to be one for the record books because the two of you have wonderful chemistry and within hours of meeting declared Intent to begin a Formal Courtship. It will be considered a love story for the ages. The bards will speak of how you looked upon one another and fell in love at first sight. They'll talk of how you began a quest to win approval from the North Wind." The being declared.

"I didn't fall in love at first sight. I decided to declare Intent after Arith explained all the reasons I would make a good suitor and watching Arith threaten those two sealed the deal for me." Izal explained.

"Well, you are an Ifrit. Being told that you're a good prospective mate flattered you but watching your potential bondmate threatening an enemy would've been intoxicating." The being explained.

"Arith caught fire and advanced towards them. I smiled and told Arith that I would consider attacking them a suitable courting gift. Arith immediately calmed down and asked if I meant that I was willing to court them. So I declared my Intent. There's no way I was going to let a Sylph willing to set their enemies on fire get away. Especially not after being told they viewed me as a potential suitor." Izal said, smiling at Arith.

"Must you two bond over your desire to set me on fire?" Dennis whined.

"Yes." Arith, Izal and the robed being said in unison.

"Izal do you stand by your Intent to enter into a Formal Courtship with Arith? Do you understand what shall be expected of you in this Courtship?"

"I am Izal Sunbound and it is my Intent to enter into a Formal Courtship with Arith, Sylph and grandchild of the North Wind. This I declare before all here that anyone who hears may know that my troth is true. It is my hope that we shall grow closer as we journey to undo the ritual that bound me to Arith's body that I might one day be bound to Arith's heart and soul instead." Izal vowed.

The being stared for a moment. Rarely had an Intent to enter into a Formal Courtship sounded so much like a formal bonding vow. It would be interesting to see Arith's response to Izal's impromptu vows.

"Arith; Sylph and grandchild to the North Wind do you stand by your Intent to enter into a Formal Courtship with Izal Sunbound? Do you understand what shall be expected of you in this courtship?" The being asked.

"I am Arith; Sylph and grandchild to the North Wind it is my Intent to enter into a Formal Courtship with Izal Sunbound. This I declare before all here, that anyone who hears shall know my troth is true. I hope to learn more about Izal and grow closer to them as we journey to undo the ritual that bound me to Izal's body that I might one day be bound to Izal's heart and soul instead." Arith vowed.

The being smiled. "Then by the powers vested in me I declare the Formal Courtship of Izal and Arith official. May your years together be many and the love you feel for each other grow with each passing day."

Arith and Izal smiled at each other and for a moment they forgot that they still had a quest to solve and basked in the glow of the other's smile.

"Was that normal?" Greg asked Dennis as quietly as he could.

"No. I've never seen two individuals enter into a Formal Courtship with such weight behind their promises. If they don't end up as lifemates after this I'll be shocked." Dennis admitted.

Chapter 8
Flaming Tornado

They left the temple in silence. After awhile, Izal spoke up. "Is there anywhere in particular you think we should go from here?" they asked.

"You promised me food." Dennis insisted.

"There should be a marketplace nearby. They'll have something you can eat. Just remember to stay in character." Izal warned.

"What character? Greg's a Zombie."

"That's rude. I'm Undead, not a Zombie. Besides, you don't hear me complaining about your body." Greg retorted.

"Why would anyone complain about being me? I'm a god. Being me rocks. Being you on the other hand sucks."

Arith watched them squabbling and felt rage boiling over. "I warned you not to fight again. This is the last straw. It's time for the two of you to learn to knock it off. I don't care who started it, I will finish it. Izal, would you be a dear and help me teach these two the error of their ways?"

Izal smirked. "Sure thing. It'll be a nice bonding opportunity for us. Watching our powers interact will be interesting. I've been wanting to set them on fire since shortly after I woke up. Just remember anger will summon flames. I'll try and recreate the tornado from earlier."

Arith burst into flames and shortly after Izal summoned a small tornado. Arith and Izal added flames to the tornado and moved it towards the squabbling duo who were unaware of the danger they were in.

The air around Dennis and Greg began to heat up and they looked around, finding themselves surrounded by a fiery tornado. "We warned you not to fight any longer. Now you'll have to deal with the consequences," Izal and Arith intoned.

"You can't kill us. You need us alive to undo the ritual," Dennis exclaimed.

"We don't know that. Even if it's true there's no guarantee we need you in one piece. I think I could survive remaining permanently body-swapped," Izal added.

"You wouldn't really leave us to die would you?" Greg questioned.

"I think we've made it very clear what we're willing to do to get some peace and quiet." Arith retorted.

Dennis stared at the fiery tornado, his earlier bravado leaving faster than the flames as they moved towards him. Just before he would've started begging

Izal stepped in.

"I think they've learned their lesson. Besides I don't think anyone here wants to know what barbecued Zombie smells like," Izal said, turning to Arith.

Arith's nose scrunched up in disgust. "Yuck! That is a thought I really didn't need."

"I'm sorry. I thought I could handle it but the thought of that smell sickened me," Izal admitted.

Greg looked like he wanted to comment on being called a Zombie but seemed to think having his original body burned was worse than the insult.

"Any chance we could get back to finding food?" Dennis asked once the flames vanished.

CHAPTER 9
THE MARKETPLACE

They entered the marketplace and did their best not to stare. The variety in species and wares was staggering. Even Izal seemed mildly impressed.

"The place has grown since I was last here. I'll have to see if my family's stall is still here. My cousin Bowie used to sell the best curry in the Underworld. It'll make you believe in all nine levels of Dante's Inferno," Izal promised.

"Do you think your cousin would be willing to feed us?" Greg asked.

"Certainly. I'll have to inform my family of my courtship and the events preceding it but after that they'll give us food. If we're lucky they'll decide to hold a feast to celebrate my finding a worthy suitor," Izal said, smiling at the thought.

"What if they don't like me?" Arith asked.

"They'll adore you. Once they find out that you managed to summon flames after being an Ifrit for less than a day they'll be begging you to join the family. Some of my relatives might try to lure you into a courtship with them," Izal replied.

"Why would they want to break our courtship?" Arith asked.

"To ensure you stayed in the family even if things didn't work out between us. Finding an elemental willing to bond with an Ifrit is difficult. They'll appreciate your fire. A bonding like ours doesn't happen often and when it does it's considered cause for celebration. Trust me they'll love you," Izal promised.

"I don't want anyone else in your family. Just you,"

Arith declared with a pout.

Izal chuckled. "I'm glad. I don't think I'd enjoy seeing you making eyes at my cousins or worse,my siblings."

"Oh, so it's fine for your family to make eyes at me but not for me to make eyes at them," Arith growled, flames flickering into existence.

"I didn't say I'd like my family attempting to court you, just that I thought they would. I told you my family would approve so you'd stop being nervous. Besides, it can't be news to you that you're a worthy suitor. I'm sure I'm not the first to try and win you over," Izal insisted.

Arith blushed. "I haven't had much time for suitors. Between my grandfather and the scandal I've had a remarkable dearth of prospective bondmates."

"Their loss is my gain. I can't help it if everyone around you was ignorant. Anyone unwilling to brave your family or risk the rumor mill is unworthy of you. By the time they realize what they missed out on it'll be too late," Izal declared.

"If you keep talking like that you won't have to worry about whether or not my grandfather likes you. He'd never try to prevent me from being with someone who defends me so adamantly. Even my parents aren't that ardent in my defense," Arith admitted.

"You sure you don't want me to try and whip up some revenge on your behalf? My family will help. Dennis would help if it meant you forgave him," Izal bargained.

"Sure thing. I'm all for a bit of revenge once I'm back in my own body. Especially if it means I never have to worry about fiery tornadoes again," Dennis added.

"I don't know. My parents mean well. They just don't understand me. I'm too serious for them and they're used to doing what other people tell them." Arith admitted.

"They're your parents. They're supposed to love you, not the idea of you." Greg insisted. "Love isn't supposed to contain limits or only show up when convenient. I'm sure your grandfather doesn't try to make you into someone you're not. If the North Wind doesn't think you need to change to be loved, why do your parents?" Greg asked.

"We don't have to stay if you don't want to. We'll meet with my family, get some food and see if they have any suggestions for how to fix this. If you feel uncomfortable just claim you need to talk to your grandfather and we'll leave," Izal suggested.

"Okay. Let's do this," Arith said, smiling at Izal. "Thanks for understanding."

"It's fine. I'm just glad you're willing to meet my family."

"I was going to wind up meeting them at some point anyway. I just wasn't expecting to meet them the day we started courting," Arith admitted, trying to play it cool.

"True, but nothing about our courtship was ever going to be normal. We met for the first time after being body swapped and then started courting. That's the kind of story you end up telling your grandkids. Our courtship is the stuff of legends." Izal said, trying to make Arith blush.

"You say the sweetest things," Arith said with a smile.

CHAPTER 10
SUNBOUND CURRY STALL

They wound their way through the marketplace past clothing and jewels, demons and ghouls following the scent of curry. Izal walked into the stall first motioning for the others to wait.

"Is this the stall with the famous Sunbound Curry?" Izal asked.

"Yes. I should be able to make a mild curry for a sweet thing like you," the Ifrit replied.

"Cut the crap Bowie. I'm Izal and I have no use for your philandering ways. I need to talk to Mikra. I have news for the family and not all of it is good. Fetch Mikra and I won't try and feed you to Dennis." Izal threatened.

"I don't know how you found out about Izal and Mikra but there's no way I'm bothering Mikra on your say so," Bowie argued, grabbing Izal in a chokehold.

With that Arith walked in. "Perhaps this form is more memorable. Unhand my suitor before I set you on fire." When Bowie failed to do so Arith summoned flames. "You get one more chance to set Izal down before I find out how hot flames need to be in order to burn an Ifrit. Coincidentally; that's my body you're choking and I'm not terribly thrilled to find you manhandling it," Arith threatened.

"I thought I asked you to stay behind," Izal said, looking at Arith who'd arrived without backup.

"You did and I did. I only intervened when bozo over there began choking you. Dennis and Greg agreed that a flaming tornado should be enough backup for any situation."

"What do you mean by a flaming tornado?" Bowie asked.

"Oh, that's simple. Izal can summon tornadoes while in Sylph form and I can summon flames in Ifrit form so we figured out that if we combine our powers we can make a fiery tornado of doom. Now will you let Izal go or would you like to find out first hand just how unbreakable a Fae's word really is?" Arith asked as flames began to appear.

Bowie let go of the Sylph in their hand and decided that maybe they'd been a little bit too hasty when they chose to attack instead of listen. After all, any situation that caused an Ifrit and a Sylph to team up had to be worth learning about. Especially when the Ifrit in question happened to be their wayward cousin.

CHAPTER 11
BOWIE MEETS DENNIS

"Come in. This'll be worth a few bowls of curry," Bowie offered.

"What about Dennis and Greg? Can they come in for curry as well?" Izal asked.

Bowie hesitated. "Wasn't Dennis the one you threatened to feed me too?

"Yes he was," Izal confirmed.

"Why would Dennis eat me?" Bowie asked.

"Dennis is currently in Greg's body and Greg's a Zombie. Apparently the hunger is overpowering though since all Dennis has done for the last few hours is whine about being hungry. Since Dennis appears to be in some kind of Zombie body we thought it best to feed him before he decides that we look tasty."

"Alright. I'll feed your demented guard dog. But if he makes any sudden moves I'll set him on fire." Bowie warned.

"Fair enough. We've threatened him a few times too. The whining was unbearable. Besides, it was funny to see a god cowering before something as minor as a fiery tornado," Izal admitted.

Bowie blinked, thinking about asking for clarification before deciding that it'd be easier to deal with on a full stomach with plenty of alcohol nearby in case the information needed to be forgotten later.

Izal gestured for Dennis and Greg to join them. Once the two had arrived Bowie pulled the curtains closed and put a sign up that said closed due to family emergency.

"That is an oddly specific sign," Greg commented.

"It's an Underworld staple. All the merchants have one. It cuts down on the number of customers complaining about places closing unexpectedly. I'm not sure how the magic works but the sign is always accurate. The family wasn't certain the sign would help but business picked up once customers knew we weren't lying about why we closed up." Bowie said, grinning at them in a way that suggested it was their idea.

Chapter 12
Meeting with Mikra

Bowie led them to the family restaurant. "Wait here while I get Mikra. It may take a few minutes. Mikra isn't exactly my biggest fan." Bowie said before rushing off.

"How long do you think it'll take for Bowie to return with Mikra?" Arith asked.

"Depends on how much Mikra dislikes Bowie and whether or not Mikra's curiosity can overpower that dislike," Izal explained.

"That still doesn't tell me how long we'll be

waiting," Arith said, glaring at Izal.

"Mikra may not always understand me but I don't think I'm hated. Once Bowie explains that I'm waiting to talk with the family over curry and I've brought a Sylph, a god and a Zombie with me Mikra should arrive fairly quickly. We'll probably end up waiting for about an hour. I am curious though about why Bowie thinks Mikra isn't fond of them. Last time I visited, Bowie was the favored child. That's why they ended up running the stall," Izal admitted.

"Were you sad when the stall went to Bowie?" Arith asked.

"No. I like cooking but for me it's more about being close to a flame than a desire to feed everyone. I'm also not mercenary enough to be a merchant. I'm more likely to give food away than sell it. I would've been a terrible choice."

"That still doesn't tell me if you were sad you didn't wind up chosen," Arith insisted.

"I understood why they chose Bowie to run the

stall but it was sadder that I wasn't given the option of working in any of the family restaurants. I didn't want to but sometimes it felt like they didn't trust me enough to let me work in the family business," Izal admitted.

Footsteps sounded behind them and everyone turned to look as Bowie walked in with an older Ifrit.

"You would've been miserable in days. There was no need to offer you a job you didn't want or need. We weren't trying to kick you out of the family. You did fairly well for yourself and we're proud to call you kin. It's better that you found your own way instead of resenting us for holding you back." Mikra insisted.

"I wish someone had bothered to tell me that. All I knew was that no-one wanted me working with them and I was being encouraged to leave," Izal admitted.

"If you'd talked to us we'd have told you that wasn't true. How long have you been holding this in child?" Mikra asked.

"Since the day I left," Izal whispered, staring at the ground.

"You left the day after graduating from demon school. You were still working on controlling your flames. We thought you left because you wanted to make your own way in the world. We never would've let you go if we thought it wasn't what you wanted. It's not our way to force our younglings out," Mikra insisted, eyes glistening.

"Sweetheart; you said you were being encouraged to leave. Who convinced you not to stay?" Arith asked.

Mikra and Bowie gasped and small flames began to wink into existence. "My teachers said they'd never seen a Sunbound take so long to master flames. They said I didn't have the right to wield the name. They called me halfling. Said my bearer must've been quite hard up if they chose to mate outside the species. I burned the first one who suggested they could sire a proper Ifrit with my bearer," Izal spat.

"I don't blame you. If you'd told me I'd have burned down the school. Just remember we're demons and when we decide to get vengeance everyone will remember why they shouldn't mess with the Sunbound Clan," Mikra swore.

"You're not mad at me?" Izal asked.

"No, child. I'm not mad at you. I'm angry that a place we trusted with our children betrayed us and tried to drive away one of my grandchildren. Don't worry I'll deal with the school later. But first, why don't you explain who's calling you sweetheart and why you came to see me," Mikra suggested.

CHAPTER 13
ANNOUNCING THE COURTSHIP

"I was forced into a four pointed star earlier and used for a ritual that stole my magic and knocked me unconscious along with Arith, Greg and Dennis. When I woke up I found out all of us had swapped bodies. Dennis and Greg switched and Arith and I switched. While traveling Arith said I would make a good suitor. Once Arith summoned flames and threatened Dennis with them I declared Intent. We stopped at a Temple on the way here and began our official courtship. I hoped that if I stopped by you'd feed us and offer advice," Izal explained with a sheepish grin.

"Of course we'll help. You've come home and you brought this charming Sylph with you to meet the family. Your parents will be thrilled. We'll need to hold a feast. It's never good to plot revenge on an empty stomach," Mikra said, motioning for everyone to follow.

They stepped further into the stall and entered a portal. When they exited the portal they were in Mikra's home. "Inform the family that I expect them all here for dinner." Mikra says to the first Ifrit they see. "Izal has come home and we have much to discuss. I have to start cooking if I want the feast to be ready in time," Mikra says to themself.

Dennis' stomach makes an ungodly sound and Mikra hurries to grab some leftover curry to stave off the zombie's ravenous nature. "You're a guest in my home. You can't eat people, it's impolite," Mikra insists, handing over the curry.

Dennis nods and begins to eat; the curry is gone too soon but the growling stops. Everyone breathes a sigh of relief.

"Would you like help?" Izal asks and Mikra smiles.

"Yes. Do you know if any of our guests can cook?" Mikra asks.

"I thought non-clan members weren't allowed to learn the recipe for the famous Sunbound Curry," Izal teased.

"Arith's courting you. They're practically family. Besides, this will give me a chance to get to know your suitor," Mikra replied laughing as Izal blushed.

Arith smiled and walked over to Mikra. "It would be my pleasure. Just let me know what you need." Arith said as the three of them walked into the kitchen.

"Try not to break anything," Izal said glaring at Dennis and Greg before leaving the room.

CHAPTER 14
THE FEAST

They walked into the dining room. The tantalizing smells reached them first. Bowie motioned for Greg and Dennis to take their seats. Mikra came over and ushered Izal and Arith to the seats across from Izal's parents.

After everyone had been seated Mikra spoke. "We are here to celebrate the formal courtship of Izal and Arith. Let us eat and get to know our newest clan member. We'll talk afterwards," Mikra said before filling their plate.

Arith's eyes widened. "But I'm not a member of your clan," Arith whispered.

Izal's smirked. "Not yet; but you will be if I have anything to say about it." They promised, causing Arith to blush.

Izal's parents smiled at the happy couple. "It's so nice to see our Izal all grown up and starting a family. We were starting to wonder if they would ever bring someone home to meet us." Izal's bearer teased.

"Arith this is my bearer Keegan and my Sire Aidan," Izal said, pointing to their parents.

"It's a pleasure to meet the one who's stolen our youngest's heart," Keegan said, giving Arith a warm smile.

"Youngest, how many siblings does Izal have?" Arith asked.

"Hasn't Izal told you about their family?" Aidan asked.

"We haven't known each other long. Arith told me I'd make a good suitor. When they tried to light Dennis on fire using my flames I knew I wanted to bond with them. The fact that we're stuck in each other's bodies for the time being just makes it easier." Izal admitted.

"That's so sweet. Stories will be told of your bonding for generations. We haven't had an Elemental in the family in eons. Arith is going to fit in perfectly just make sure to warn them about Kieran. I love Kieran but everyone knows Kieran's a flirt. I'd hate to see your intended leave because your sibling got handsy." Keegan said, smiling at them.

"If Kieran lays one hand on me then sibling or not I'll make sure they face a flaming tornado." Izal threatened.

"Any particular reason your sibling would need to worry about flaming tornadoes?" Aidan asked.

"It's what happens when we combine our powers but if it makes you feel better we can always threaten Kieran with Arith's grandfather." Izal suggested.

"I know I'm going to regret this but who is Arith's grandfather and why do you think threatening Kieran with him is similar to being attacked by a flaming tornado?" Aidan asked.

"Arith's grandfather is the North Wind." Izal explained.

Aidan rubbed their temples, sighed really loudly and paused before speaking. "I never thought I'd say this but the flaming tornado is kinder. You can't threaten Kieran with Arith's grandfather unless they put their hands on one of you. I'll try to speak to your siblings so they know not to behave badly." Aidan promised.

"Enough of this seriousness. It's a feast. We're meant to be eating, drinking and celebrating. We'll worry about all of that later." Keegan said before piling food on their plate. With that said they all began to enjoy the feast.

Arith smiled when they looked at their plate to see that they were each served Manzanita Flower Tea. "Make sure you add a decent amount of sweet dishes and desserts. Elementals convert sugar into energy and use that to replenish their magic. Do you have any dietary requirements I should know about dear heart?" Arith asked.

"Start with the curry. I've yet to find a dish too spicy for a Sunbound. Anything you see should be delicious. Mikra wouldn't let anyone serve a dish they didn't approve of at an event they're hosting." Izal said, smiling at Arith.

They dug in and once all of the food had been devoured Mikra stood up. "I must confess the feast, while delicious, was not the only reason I asked everyone to come. Izal was used in a ritual without their consent and while it led them to their Intended that does not mean I approve. Izal and their Intended Arith have asked for help finding out who did this to them and how to fix it. I'd like everyone to take the time to relax and meet me in the living room in an hour to discuss what to do next." Mikra said in a tone that brooked no argument.

CHAPTER 15
SUNBOUND WAR COUNCIL

When everyone finally gathered in the living room Izal noticed that Kieran was sitting as far away from them and Arith as possible. This wouldn't have been noteworthy if it weren't for the fact that Kieran had made the unfortunate decision to sit next to Dennis. From the look on Kieran's face they were also struggling to decide whether or not setting a zombie on fire was worth the smell.

Izal shook their head. This wasn't the time to get sidetracked. Their family had gathered together to support them and ignoring their efforts would be rude. Izal watched as Mikra walked in and commanded attention.

"Does anyone have any suggestions for how to help Izal?" Mikra asked.

"Arith's grandfather would probably help if we asked him." Izal suggested.

"Why do you think we should contact Arith's grandfather?" Mikra asked.

"Arith's grandfather is the North Wind. He either knows what happened already or he will shortly. I also don't want to be accused of keeping this from him. I don't feel like getting on his bad side." Izal admitted.

"Arith do you have any suggestions for how to contact your grandfather?" Mikra asked.

"If I know my grandfather he knows what happened already and is just waiting for me to ask for his help. He won't interfere unless I ask him to. Now that I've mentioned wanting help he'll contact me soon. Nothing's faster than a rumor on the wind." Arith said with a smile.

"I see. Do you know what help he'll give?" Mikra asked.

"That depends on how much information he's able to find before he contacts me. Worst case scenario the being or beings who engineered this can't be crossed by him and he'll tell me he can't help. But I think it's more likely he'll give me information and his blessing on my quest. If Izal impresses him my grandfather might offer us a courting gift which we can use on the quest." Arith admitted.

"That's good to know. Does anyone else have any suggestions?" Mikra asked. When the silence had gone on long enough to become awkward Mikra glared. "Izal came to us for help. Do I have to come up with all the ideas around here?" Mikra demanded throwing their hands up in exasperation.

"Scrying should be able to find the ritual site where Izal, Arith and the other two got swapped." Dante suggested causing Izal to smile at their sibling.

"We have names you know." Dennis insisted.

"Yeah, but none of us care." Kieran retorted.

"If you two are done squabbling like spoiled children we can get back to the important things." Mikra said, lashing them with the sharp side of their tongue.

"Sorry Mikra." Kieran said, hanging their head in shame.

Dennis looked like he didn't want to apologize but Mikra's glare convinced him otherwise. "Sorry." Dennis said when flames began to appear in Mikra's hands.

"There's a soothsayer in the Marketplace. They owe me a favor so don't let them charge you for it. Let them know I sent you. I'll make sure to send you a couple care packages before you leave. The day's almost over so you should stay here for the night and continue your quest in the morning." Mikra said before ushering them off to their temporary sleeping quarters.

CHAPTER 16
Last Minute Advice

After a satisfying breakfast Izal, Arith, Dennis and Greg met Mikra in the living room. "Well darlings. It's been lovely having you stay with us. Take care of Izal for me will you Arith. I expect an invitation to your bonding." Mikra smiled at the courting couple before turning a glare on the last members of their party.

"I better not hear that you two knuckleheads injured my grandchildren. Stop fighting all the time and work together or you're going to have a lot more problems than just being body-swapped. Not everyone's as understanding as I am. It doesn't matter how much power you used to have. As long as you're trapped like this you won't be able to do anything about it. Besides, even if you do get your powers back it doesn't mean you won't encounter someone with more, who doesn't like your attitude." Mikra warned.

Greg looked like he wanted to argue but thought it wouldn't help. Dennis on the other hand was fuming. Knuckles clenched he looked ready to pound Mikra's face in.

Izal stepped in front of Dennis. "If you do anything to Mikra it will violate the laws of hospitality. Mikra would be well within their rights to banish you from the premises and depending on the severity of your crimes could declare a blood feud. I'd support them and as Arith is my intended, so would they. We've got no problem leaving Greg in your body or abandoning both of you if it comes to it. So think real hard before you do something you'll regret because if you don't none of us will regret our revenge." Izal promised Arith's sweet voice a direct contrast to the blatant threat.

"Izal's right. Consider this your last warning Dennis. After this you're on your own. I've done what I could to help the four of you but if we need to we can find a way to alter the ritual so it requires two or three people instead of the original four." Mikra said before handing over the packages and ushering them out the door.

The look Mikra gave Izal and Arith said that any longer in Dennis' presence and they would've said or done something they couldn't take back. With a final wave the four of them left in search of the soothsayer.

CHAPTER 17
MEETING THE SOOTHSAYER

"If I remember correctly Madame Zelazny's stall is on the Eastern edge of the market." Izal remarked before leading the group in the right direction.

It took them very little time to reach their destination. "Izal, Arith, it's good to see you both. Congratulations on your courtship. If everyone involved can remember the questing rules there's no reason this can't end happily for everyone involved." Madame Zelazny warned. For some reason the demonic soothsayer seemed to glare at Dennis as she said that.

"Why are you glaring at me? I haven't done anything." Dennis said, voice rising in irritation.

"Yes, you have. There've been numerous warnings over the course of this quest about your arrogance. You know your mouth is writing checks your magic can't cash right now. Nobody's going to care about the power you used to have. At this rate no-one's going to help you." Madame Zelazny warned.

Dennis tried to say something but Greg hit him over the head with a frying pan knocking him out. "Where did you get the frying pan?" Izal asked.

"Mikra gave it to me last night. They told me it was my job to keep Dennis from insulting Madame Zelazny if I wanted to get my body back. I figured if I hit Dennis hard enough they would be mad enough at me to keep from offending anyone else." Greg admitted.

"You weren't worried about hurting your body?" Arith asked.

"I've woken up from worse. Besides, haven't you noticed Madame Zelazny's warning? She told us this would only end happily for everyone if we all behaved. She didn't say one of us misbehaving would ruin things for everyone. She was trying to get Dennis and I to understand that if we're not careful our quests will end badly. You two are almost certain to wind up better off than you were simply because of how you've acted so far," Greg explained.

"Well said. Since the idiot's not going to wake up for a while; I'd like to have a private chat with Greg if you don't mind. I believe the stall on my right should have some hygiene charms that will help on your quest," Madame Zelazny suggested softly ushering Izal and Arith out the door.

CHAPTER 18
DAMMIT DENNIS

After acquiring the charms Madame Zelazny recommended and browsing for half an hour Greg came and got them. "Madame Zelazny said I couldn't tell you what we talked about without decreasing the odds of finishing the quest successfully. We need to grab Dennis and head south to the Unnamed River. The North Wind will meet us there." Greg explained as they walked back.

They grabbed Dennis just before he woke back up. Which was great because none of them wanted to carry him. "Why did you hit me?" Dennis asked as they shoved him out the door.

"Because you were about to insult the soothsayer we asked for help. The fact that you're an arrogant jackweasel just made it easier. Besides, this way you have options. Izal and Arith can attack you with a flaming tornado when you piss them off or I can hit you with this," Greg said, pulling the frying pan out of his backpack.

"Aren't you worried about giving yourself brain damage?" Dennis asked.

"I got run over by a garbage truck once. Wound up in the hospital after I broke every bone in my body and pulverized my internal organs. I was back to work in three days and fully healed four days after that. The fact that you don't have a concussion right now despite me hitting you hard enough to knock you unconscious should be reassuring," Greg said and for the first time they truly believed Greg had earned the name Savage.

"Not gonna lie Greg. I respect you a lot more now

that I know that," Izal said as Arith nodded in agreement.

"...Thank you." Greg said, rubbing the back of his head.

"Madame Zelazny recommended these charms for our journey," Izal said as they passed them out to everyone.

"What do they do?" Dennis asked.

"They're hygiene charms. We won't need to stop as frequently since magic will ensure we don't have to worry about it. They speed up our metabolism by converting food and drink into energy which we can use for endurance or magic," Izal explained.

"Ooookay. Are there any side effects?" Dennis asked.

"Sure. You might experience more minor magical outbursts but I thought it would be preferable to having someone else take your body to the bathroom like a child," Izal said.

Dennis shuddered. "Thank you. I hadn't thought of

that. I don't want to find out how Greg's body works," Dennis insisted, shuddering again at the thought.

Greg looked angry but seemed to think about it for a moment then shook his head. "We should get going if we want to reach the Unnamed River before nightfall," Greg suggested walking south.

They made good time and reached the river by midday. The charms were already helping. Izal knew it would normally have taken a full day to reach the river and they'd done it in a matter of hours. Luckily the charms were sold with spells to ease muscle soreness or they'd all be feeling the effects of moving at that speed by now.

"We should eat soon. Dennis is giving me that look again; the one which says I'd make an acceptable meal," Arith said.

Izal turned around and glared. "Next time just ask for a snack break or try to forage while we're traveling. For Flame's sake you could ask Greg to summon food for you. For all we know the magic involved in conjuring food will sustain you. Go talk to Greg about his dietary needs and try not to consume any flesh while you're in his body. None of us want to deal with the fallout," Izal insisted, shoving Dennis at Greg.

Greg dragged Dennis further away and they had a short muffled argument. Arith normally would've tried to listen but figured their grandfather would tell them later if they needed to know.

When the two came back it was clear that Greg won the argument although not before Dennis wrung some concessions out of him. "I'll try and see if I can summon various food types and Dennis has promised to avoid eating anything he knows is sentient. He refuses to believe all life forms are sentient but at least he won't eat anything he knows has a culture and a language," Greg explained.

"Did you seriously have to explain to Dennis why you didn't want him to commit cannibalism using your body?" Arith asked.

"I also had to explain to him that I prefer my food

to not be alive when it's given to me. I've threatened to hit him with Mikra's Frying Pan of Justice if he tries to eat anything that's still moving or talking when he puts it in his mouth. You might want to remind him what a flaming tornado looks like up close and personal. I smacked him because he was saying he thought Sylph would taste better than Ifrit," Greg explained.

It was at this rather disastrous moment that Greg realized everyone's jaws had dropped for a reason and he turned around to see the North Wind summoning the mother of all tornadoes.

"Grandfather. Allow me to introduce my intended Izal. I'm sure you've worked out what happened by now. Please let me deal with Dennis for now. You can always torture him once we've gotten our rightful bodies back. At the moment the worst thing you can do to Dennis is leave him in Greg's body and hope this will help curb his arrogance and abrasive attitude." Arith said, holding Izal's hand in theirs.

"Arith you always were a rare one; not many would

stand up to me in that state. Now can you cut the formality? You know you don't need to use my title grandchild." The North Wind replied letting the tornado dissipate as he opened his arms for a hug.

"Of course Papa North. I just needed to make sure you didn't do too much damage to Greg's body. It's not fair to make Greg pay for Dennis' crimes." Arith insisted before launching themself into North's arms.

"Alright darling. I'll do my best but I will get my revenge on Dennis eventually. You know immortals don't let slights like that stand forever," North reminded Arith.

"Neither do Fae or Demons. Izal and I will do our best to keep Dennis in line. If he'd actually tried to eat me or my intended I would've burned him to a crisp and let Izal scatter the ashes," Arith promised.

Dennis shuddered even when the Sylph was protecting him; they still reminded him that they could kill him at any time. "I wouldn't have actually done it. I'm not that stupid," Dennis muttered.

"Of course not. I'd have killed you myself if I thought you were going to use my body to murder someone and eat the corpse." Greg reminded him hefting Mikra's Frying Pan of Justice in a menacing manner.

"We can threaten Dennis later. I'd like to get back to my own body so I can continue courting Arith." Izal insisted with a small blush.

"I like you, Izal. You've been taking great care of my grandchild, threatening their enemies and you can cook. It doesn't mean I'm ready to give you my blessing but it does help," North said, patting Izal on the shoulder.

"With all due respect sir, I don't need your permission or approval to court Arith or protect them. I would appreciate your approval because it matters to Arith but the only one whose permission and approval I need is Arith's," Izal insisted, hoping it wouldn't anger the mercurial being or their intended.

North laughed. "Good. If you felt differently I'd

worry Arith had chosen poorly. Anyone wanting to bond with one of my grandchildren should know that their intended's opinion is the only one that matters. In fact I suspect the only reason Arith insists that a suitor get my blessing is to ensure they are never forced into a bonding they didn't want," North explained when Izal's eyes widened in confusion.

"That's not entirely true. I also respect your opinion and unlike the rest of my family you'd make sure that my suitor wasn't using me to get to you. You've always done your best to ensure that your descendents are safe and happy. The only beings who've ever bonded into the family under false pretenses are the ones you didn't approve of. I want you to make sure that I never make an impulsive decision with lasting consequences," Arith explained.

"Darling, when will you learn that your family is wrong about you? You are more like me than them. I'm sorry for that. It's certainly not made life easy for you. You're more grounded than them," North explained.

"They wander from place to place. Constantly moving and going wherever the wind blows them. I rotate. Just because I stay in one city doesn't mean I wind up stagnant or hate to travel. I spend my winters somewhere different every year and I make it to every family function I'm invited to. I've learned to paint, earned degrees and am constantly learning. If I was really as staid as they think I wouldn't have done any of it," Arith insisted.

"I know. I ask the wind to keep an eye on you. You know you're my favorite," North insisted, booping Arith's nose.

"Just as you're mine," Arith insisted, giving North a massive hug.

"Always dear heart. Now for Air's sake let's get the important stuff out of the way. I hate being formal with my family. Next time I see you it better be to inform me of your intent to bond with Izal." North insisted.

"I'll do my best to make that happen." Arith promised.

North smiled. "This happened for a lot of reasons but the long and short of it is that I can't tell you what I know right now. Everyone involved has their own reasons for doing this and some effort was made to do it in the way with the most positive outcomes possible. If Dennis eats anyone or tries to eat anyone in Greg's body they will lose their godhood forever and become a chew toy for eternity. If Greg fails to heed the warnings he'll wind up worse than dead. Right now none of the seers, soothsayers or oracles have seen you or Izal come to bad ends. If that changes, whoever's fate they've seen will also receive a warning. Remember to obey the questing rules and everyone will get a happy ending." North promised before fading away leaving behind nothing but a cool breeze.

CHAPTER 19
HERE WE GO AGAIN

"**W**hat are the questing rules?" Greg asked.

"Obey the rules of Hospitality and it will never backfire. If someone gives you advice during a quest no matter how strange, follow it. Be respectful whenever possible. You never know how powerful someone is unless they choose to tell you. Don't anger a dragon if you can avoid it. If you run into a stranger on a quest they will either help or harm you in most cases that's determined by how you treat them.

Honesty will get you much farther than lies. Each quest member must change in some way in order for the quest to be successful. Otherwise grocery trips would count as quests. Avoid arrogance and no invoking of deities without proper sacrifice," Izal explained.

"There are a lot of rules. I'm not sure I can remember all of them," Greg admitted.

"Most of them boil down to two things. Every quest rule except for one boils down to either safety or respect. That rule is usually ignored. Not because it doesn't matter but because it's the one rule no-one can affect. Nothing anyone does will keep a quest from changing them in some way," Izal explained.

"That helps. Does anyone have any idea where we should go next?" Greg asked, sounding relieved.

"We should follow the river. We're near the southern edge of the Underworld and the Unnamed River leads us out of this realm. Quest magic should take over if we get too far off track as long as we follow the rules and don't split up," Izal suggested.

They followed the river until it led to a portal. Since no-one appeared to stop them from going through it the group went through. When they arrived Izal smiled. "This looks like the Demon Realm. I've lived here for sixteen years but it changes frequently so stay close. Hopefully we'll run into someone I know so we can ask for help or at least gather supplies." Izal suggested.

Before long Izal found themself on a very familiar street. "That's my apartment. I'm going to make sure no-one's sold it while I was gone but it looks like we'll have somewhere to sleep tonight and we should be able to resume traveling in the morning." Izal suggested as they gestured to the ever darkening sky.

"It doesn't feel like we walked that long," Greg muttered.

"That's because of the charms. When you stop moving you'll feel exhausted. There should be a few extra beds if my roommate's are out of town again but if not you can crash on the couch or the floor. The charms should keep you comfortable and it'll be much safer than sleeping outdoors." Izal said, walking up to the door.

Izal knocked and when they heard no response they turned to Arith. "Would you mind handing me the key in your pocket?" Izal asked.

Arith handed over the black key and Izal unlocked the door. "Welcome to my home. I'm going to see if my roommate's left me any contact information." Izal said, ushering them inside.

"It's nice." Arith said, looking around at the cozy apartment. "How many roommates do you have?" Arith asked.

"Three but they work a lot so most of the time I'm the only one home." Izal admitted and made a beeline for the note on the fridge. Izal read the note. "Looks like they won't be back for a few days but Zane might be stopping by." Izal said with a smile.

"Who's Zane?" Arith asked.

"Zane's the only one of my siblings you haven't

met yet. You'll like them. They usually show up a few times a year trying to convince me to come home or at least explain why I left," Izal explained.

"Then I hope we get to meet Zane before we leave," Arith said.

"There's toiletries in the bathroom if you want to take a shower and clean clothes in my room which is at the end of the hall on the left. You should take my bed." Izal suggested.

"You don't have to give up your bed," Arith insisted.

"I'm not having my Intended sleep in my roommate's bed and I'm not ready to share a bed yet. Besides, no other bed is big enough for you," Izal said, gesturing to their giant frame.

Arith sighed. "Okay. I'll sleep in your bed but don't blame me if I burn your sheets," Arith warned.

"Considering how many sets of sheets I went through, that's fair. I'm gonna go make sure the trouble twins are settling in okay." Izal said walking away.

After everyone settled in for the night, they all went to their respective rooms to sleep. Each of them hoped that tomorrow would bring them closer to a solution.

Chapter 20
Demon Den

In the middle of the night there was a loud sound that woke everyone up. "What did you guys do to my apartment?" Izal demanded once the four of them had gathered in the living room.

"Nothing." Greg, Dennis and Arith replied.

"One of you must've done something." Izal insisted.

"I don't care who did what. I'm tired and I want to sleep. We can deal with it in the morning. The next person to wake me up is getting set on fire." Arith insisted before heading back to bed.

"You better not have broken anything." Izal threatened, glaring at the troublesome two as they all collectively decided to get more sleep.

The next time they woke up it was hours later and they gathered in the kitchen. "There's cereal if you two want some." Izal offered before making Challah French Toast for them and Arith.

"Why aren't you making us breakfast?" Dennis asked.

"It's my house and my food. Arith's my Intended so of course I'll cook for them besides I don't want you touching my cookware. There's spoons, bowls and cereal laid out for you. Use them or don't eat." Izal retorted, turning back to the food.

Dennis immediately turned green, ran off and upchucked violently in the bathroom.

Greg stared in disbelief. "I didn't know people could actually turn green. His skin's the same color as the neon sign outside the bar I work in." Greg said in horrified fascination.

"Huh. Wonder what happened to him?" Izal mused before handing Arith their food and cooking their own. Minutes later they were eating their breakfast and ignoring Dennis as usual. Neither of the courting couple noticed Greg looking pale and weak.

When breakfast was over they heard a knock at the door. Arith opened the door and the newcomer walked in before turning around with a nasty glare and a fireball in each hand. "Who are you and what did you do to my sibling?" The Ifrit demanded.

"You must be Zane. If you give me a second I can ask Izal to help explain things to you." Arith suggested turning their back on Zane and walking towards the kitchen. "Izal, Zane's here and they have a few questions for us." Arith said paying no attention to the fireballs.

"How did you know?" Izal asked, staring at Zane in confusion.

"I can read auras. It's not a normal talent for

Sunbounds so I didn't want to say anything." Zane admitted. "Although that still doesn't explain why your aura isn't in your body."

"We got body-swapped by a ritual and now we're on a quest to undo the ritual and return to our normal lives. Arith and I are also courting," Izal said, giving a pointed look at the fireballs in Zane's hands.

"Ah, sorry about that. I wasn't trying to fry your Intended," Zane admitted.

"No worries. If you'd been able to make it to the family meeting Mikra called you would already know all of this," Arith explained.

"I didn't know Mikra had called a family meeting. I'll have to swing by soon and apologize for not making it," Zane said, giving Arith a big smile. "Still at least I got to meet you and help out Izal a bit."

"Well, we're certainly glad you're here. I'm sure you and Izal have lots to talk about," Arith said, walking towards the couch.

"Where are you going? As Izal's Intended what I

have to say affects you too," Zane said.

"What did you want to talk about?" Izal asked.

"I want to go into business with you," Zane blurted.

"What kind of business and why me?" Izal asked.

"A Detective Agency. With my aura reading we should be able to solve cases faster. Besides, I can't think of anyone I'd rather work with than you," Zane admitted.

"Why not ask one of our siblings to help?" Izal asked.

"I didn't want to have to tell them about my gift and I've always been closer to you anyway. They'd want to take over and they'd end up taking all the credit. Besides, do you really think any of our other siblings would be willing to take orders from either of us?" Zane asked.

"Dante would and Horatio listens to us sometimes," Izal argued.

"Okay, I'll consider Dante and if we need help we can call Horatio but I want the two of us to be the backbone of the organization," Zane insisted.

"What about Arith?" Izal asked.

"How would Arith help?" Zane asked.

"I can ask the wind to let me know what it's heard. I don't think either of you have access to that much information," Arith said with a smirk.

"Okay, but there's still a lot of things to work out. We'd need an officc, a business name, permits and licenses. There's a ton of paperwork involved in setting up your own business," Izal explained.

"I have a lead on a building. I was thinking of calling it Sunbound Investigations and I'm sure Mikra would help with the paperwork." Zane insisted.

"You've really put a lot of thought into this haven't you?" Izal asked.

"Yes," Zane replied.

"Then when we've completed our quest we'll sit down with our immediate family, Arith and Mikra before going into business together." Izal promised.

Zane smiled and looked like all of their dreams had

come true until Dennis walked in the room when their smile vanished, replaced by a confused look. "Did you know you're pregnant?" Zane asked.

"Who's pregnant?" Dennis asked.

"You are." Zane insisted.

"That's not possible. I'm a guy, guy's can't get pregnant," Dennis retorted.

"There's normally eighteen different ways to get pregnant. Being a guy isn't what should make this impossible," Zane replied.

"Huh. I was taught there are twenty-three," Arith said.

"The last five include adoption, not pregnancy. Besides, there's more but the others are so specific that nobody gets warned about them," Zane explained.

"Ah, can we get back to why you think I'm pregnant?" Dennis demanded.

"I don't think you're pregnant, I know you are. I read auras and it is showing that you're pregnant. Which is rather shocking since you're a Zombie and shouldn't be able to conceive," Zane explained.

"Uh oh," Greg muttered hoping no-one would hear them. Everyone turned to look at Greg.

"What do you mean uh oh?" Dennis asked with murder in his eyes.

"I think we figured out what caused the explosion last night. The chaos magic must have burst out of me causing the sound and the pregnancy." Greg admitted.

"How did this happen?" Dennis asked.

"I don't know. I've only had chaos magic for a few days. I haven't figured out how to control it yet," Greg admitted.

"Are they always like this?" Zane asked.

"Yes," Arith and Izal said in unison.

"Alright. That's enough. We're going to the market. Someone there should be able to confirm the pregnancy and help us figure out what to do next," Izal insisted.

Chapter 21
Demon Market

They headed west following Zane through the various roads and alleys needed to reach the Demon Market. "You'll need to see a healer and an Oracle of some kind. Which one do you want to start with?" Zane asked.

"We'll start with the healer. The sooner we find out why you think I'm pregnant, the sooner we can fix it," Dennis insisted.

"Madame Zelazny told me I needed to take responsibility for magic and if magic herself decreed that something was to be I should not argue even if it meant that I might be changed irrevocably. She warned that I might not stay the same but promised that if I followed directions things would work out. So that means there must be a way for this to turn out well," Greg insisted.

"We'll see; but I'm not promising anything," Dennis retorted.

"Now, now, mama, let's not be hasty," Izal teased.

"When I get my powers back I will murder you," Dennis threatened.

"Maybe so, but you don't have them now and the only thing keeping us from killing you is the fact that the ritual will be easier to undo with your help than without it and the babe you're carrying. You might be an ungrateful wretch I wouldn't spit on if he was on fire but the babe has done nothing wrong so I won't harm it," Izal promised, glaring at Dennis.

"I too will promise to do no harm to the babe but making it so no-one can hear you speak won't harm the babe. The wind will let me know if the baby needs our help," Arith warned.

"Alright, alright. I get it. You've got multiple ways to get back at me without having to resort to setting me on fire. Now can we please just get this over with. I'm nauseous, my back aches and I want to get back to my own body," Dennis pleaded.

"Sure, the healers' tents are on the West end. The Oracles are to the North so we'll stop by there after. If things follow the same pattern they have for the rest of this quest we'll find a portal shortly after we finish speaking with the Oracle," Izal explained as they walked on.

Half an hour later they arrived at the healers' tents. "We'll have to see if any of them specialize in dealing with mystical pregnancies or have the ability to diagnose you," Zane suggested so they kept looking before finding the right healer.

Healer Suzia's tent was cool and comforting. A warm matronly voice called from the back. "Take a seat. I'll be with you shortly." A few minutes later a Succubus walked out. "My name is Healer Suzia. What can I help you with today?" The demonic healer asked.

"He's pregnant. I was hoping you could confirm that since he didn't believe me when I told him. He also needs prenatal care since the pregnancy was mystically generated and we're not sure how or when it occurred. It might also help if you could let us know what species the babe is or might be since it'll tell us more about what the babe needs." Zane explained, pointing to Dennis.

"Okay. What's your name sir?" Healer Suzia asked before beginning her exam.

"My name is Dennis but this is Greg's body. Someone kidnapped us for a ritual that body swapped us. Since I wasn't pregnant in my body, if I'm pregnant it happened in the last seventy-two hours but since we think Greg used my Chaos magic to impregnate me there's no guarantee how far along the baby would be." Dennis admitted.

"Well, you're definitely pregnant and it happened late last night. You've been pregnant for less than twelve hours but since Zombies aren't meant to create life the babe has been draining you. I can't tell what species the babe is yet but it needs Chaos magic to grow since that's how it was created. Greg, you need to feed your child as much as possible. It'll siphon some of the Chaos around you but you need to use Chaos magic frequently in order to have a healthy child." Healer Suzia explained.

"Thank you. Do you know if there's a way to confirm who would be pregnant if the ritual was undone?" Zane asked. Dennis and Greg's eyes bulged as they looked at each other in confusion. None of them had thought of that yet.

"If it's me I'll carry the child to term and raise it as my own." Arith promised.

"I too would keep the child and ensure it was raised properly." Izal swore.

"Before you start fighting over it you might want to

know my thoughts on the subject," Healer Suzia said kindly chastising them.

"Oh. You're right. Our apologies Healer Suzia," Izal said.

"You will need to consider changing species at least until the babe is born. Otherwise you will weaken and die. It's very important that the baby receive regular infusions of Chaos magic until it is born. It will likely need doses of Chaos magic after as well but the amount required should drop especially since by then we should know what species the baby is so we can manage its needs better. If Greg and Dennis swap bodies and the baby does anything other than stay in Greg's body, it will be fine. If the Oracle indicates that Greg will carry the child to term then you must immediately begin to look into changing his species. Two lives depend on it." Healer Suzia insisted.

They stared at the Succubus. Whatever they'd expected her to say it wasn't that. "What would be the safest species for Dennis to change into right now?"

Greg asked.

"If you had control of the Chaos magic then I'd say a god of some kind. Since you don't then it needs to be a powerful creature capable of bearing a child safely. Most types of Fae and Demons can do so but you'll need to ask the Oracle for more information. For now all I can do is offer charms to help with nausea, some prenatals and a reminder to eat and drink while consuming as much chaos magic as possible," Healer Suzie admitted.

"Thank you for your help. I'll make sure to send someone by and let you know how things play out later," Greg promised.

They headed to the northern edge to meet the Oracle. They were too shocked to say anything about what had happened in the Healer's tent. Everyone was surprised Dennis hadn't asked Healer Suzia how to get rid of the babe especially Dennis. Normally he'd have complained about what an inconvenience this was but after all the work his quest-mates had gone through to ensure it would be safe for him to continue the pregnancy and the offers to carry the child he couldn't bring himself to say that he wished the babe did not exist.

Before they knew it they'd reached Oracle Alley. Zane decided to look for somewhere with a being waiting for them. Zane was surprised when a small red dragon waved at them. "I've been expecting you. Although I didn't realize you'd be coming with a questing party," The oracle admitted.

"I didn't know either until this morning although part of that is because I didn't know when I'd be seeing an Oracle," Zane admitted.

"Well, that's what I get for not confirming that appointments were happening when I expected them and with whom. I knew you'd be by and what you wanted to ask me but I forgot to verify that none of it had changed. I'll need to do a scrying once we're inside my tent," The Oracle said, laughing at themselves.

"Please make yourselves at home. I'm Oracle Oroboros. What brings you to Oracle Alley?" Oracle Oroboros asked.

"Wouldn't this be faster if you scryed first?" Dennis asked.

"Yes, but then I'd need to scry twice. First to ensure that I got the background information and a second time to get the answers to your questions," Oracle Oroboros explained.

"Dennis, Greg, Arith and I were all kidnapped and used in a ritual that body-swapped us. Unfortunately, Greg couldn't control Dennis' chaos magic and accidentally impregnated him with said chaos magic. Since Greg is a Zombie the babe wasn't supposed to exist and Healer Suzia recommended that we ask an Oracle what kind of species Dennis should be turned into in order to ensure he and the baby survive." Izal explained.

"Ah. That's interesting. Is there anything else you'd like to know?" Oracle Oroboros asked.

"If you could tell us whether we're on the right track to undoing the ritual and having a favorable outcome that would be lovely, but we'll accept any and all information you're willing to give us," Arith said with a smile.

"Oh, you are a charmer. Your Grandfather must be so proud," the Oracle said with a smile.

"I hope so but Papa North is much more charming than I am," Arith admitted, smiling as their grandfather appeared in a small gust.

"That's not true dear heart. After all, how many can say they've charmed me?" The North Wind asked.

"Very few outside of the family," Arith admitted.

"Good, now go sit with your Intended while I help Oroboros decide what species to turn Greg's body into and how to help Greg feed the babe," The North Wind insisted.

Arith walked over to Izal and cuddled their Intended. Under normal circumstances Arith would be cheerfully curled up in their Intended's lap but since

Izal was currently smaller than them they hauled Izal into their lap instead. Izal yelped in surprise but settled back into the surprisingly comfortable cuddle while everyone else discussed what to do next.

Greg came over. "Do you want to come over and watch my body's final transformation? Dennis is going to take a potion that should turn my body human. Oroboros doesn't remember exactly how the potion works, just that it will turn anything into a human and won't harm the child," Greg explained.

Izal reluctantly got out of Arith's lap and they walked over to watch. Once everyone was there Oroboros handed Dennis the potion. "Drink up. The sooner the transformation happens the safer you'll be," Oroboros warned.

"Did I really need an audience for this?" Dennis asked.

"I didn't realize you were shy. Don't gods like being in the spotlight?" Izal teased.

"Never mind," Dennis grumbled before drinking

the potion. Seconds after the potion was drunk Dennis turned green again. "Nobody told me humanity tasted like wet socks and hairballs," Dennis whined.

"Oh, quit whining. This is a historic event. A Zombie regained its humanity to protect its unborn child." Arith teased.

Whatever response Dennis might have had was overtaken by the transformation. He glowed as his body slowly became less grey and skeletal looking. When the glowing stopped his skin was a soft brown and he grew an afro. Dennis looked down at his body. "Greg did you know you were black?" Dennis asked.

"Why is that the first thing you commented on?" Arith asked shaking their head in disbelief.

"I was sickly, grey, and disturbingly skinny a few minutes ago. Greg's not bad looking as a human. I still wouldn't sleep with him but I'm not ashamed to be walking around in his body anymore." Dennis replied, making everyone face palm in unison including the dragon.

"Please stop commenting on my body. It's disturbing," Greg said, looking uncomfortable.

"Alright we're getting a bit off track. There's lots to do so you guys need to head west and you'll receive more information later. Zane will stay with me. We have lots to talk about," Oroboros said before ushering them off.

Chapter 22
Dice and Warnings

They left Oracle Alley and headed west for a little while before reaching a portal. They walked through and Arith gasped. "We're in the Fae Realm. The portals have always dropped us near where we need to be so I think we'll find a marketplace soon," Arith suggested.

Upon hearing no objections they continued walking although everyone was a little surprised when lightning started to strike despite the lack of storm clouds. Greg blushed a bit. "That might be my fault. I've been trying to utilize chaos magic to feed the baby but I didn't think to wish for chaos that wouldn't harm anyone," Greg admitted.

"If it helps, I didn't think of it either. I doubt I could've done much better under the circumstances," Dennis said, trying to reassure Greg.

Everyone seemed shocked. This was the last thing any of them had expected. Dennis was known for being selfish and arrogant but this was the second time in a row that he'd thought of someone else. It was strange but not unwelcome. If this continued perhaps the remainder of the quest wouldn't be that bad.

Greg did his best to focus on changing the chaos magic to make something less dangerous. After all, random lightning strikes could hurt Dennis or the baby and he didn't want that. Suddenly the lightning vanished and dice began falling from the sky. Surprisingly all of the dice that looked like they would hit Dennis turned into plushie versions. "That may be the best use of Chaos Magic I've ever seen," Dennis praised, cuddling a giant D20 plushie.

"Thanks. Let me know if you feel weak and I'll do my best to cast a different kind of chaos," Greg promised happier now that Dennis wasn't being a jerk to everyone.

They continued walking until they reached the Fae Marketplace. Upon seeing the number of beings present Greg focused and all the dice turned into plushie versions and they continued on until they reached Seer's Lane.

They stopped at the first tent they saw. "I'm Caliadne, I'll be your seer today," the nymph said, ushering them inside. "There's a lot riding on this and we don't have much time. It should have taken you much longer to get to this point but you've been changing things. Until the babe was conceived the outcome was certain and it didn't bode as well for Greg and Dennis," Caliadne said.

"Why did the babe change things?" Dennis asked.

"Because without the child you had no reason to

grow up or mend your ways. Without those changes you wouldn't have a chance at a happy ending. If you can continue to act with compassion you will regain your powers. How quickly that occurs is up to you. You will need to stay with Greg until the child is born if you switch back. Without daily access to chaos magic the babe will die," Caliadne warned.

"If the babe needs us Izal and I would be willing to stand in as godparents and offer as much chaos as we could. Papa North would help if I asked. I want us to be the child's official Fae Godparents," Arith promised and Izal nodded his agreement.

"That's kind of you. It would be wise of Greg and Dennis to accept whether Dennis is offering magical help to the child or not," Caliadne suggested.

"Why aren't you questioning whether or not Greg will be involved in the child's life?" Dennis asked, stomping his foot in indignation.

"Because he's already stepping up and even allowed his species to change to ensure the babe's survival despite being an Unlife Activist. He knows the child will require your help and is willing to allow you unrestricted access to his child despite your personal relationship not being great. Greg is already being a good parent," Caliadne explained.

"I see. Is there anything else you think I should know?" Dennis asked.

"Yes but the only thing I'm allowed to tell you is to head North. Everything will be explained soon. When this is over none of you will be the same," Caliadne warned before ushering them out of her tent. She heaved a sigh of relief. She'd almost told Dennis who'd done this to him and why. If she hadn't caught herself she'd have had Ressa after her if the deities involved didn't punish her first.

CHAPTER 23
RESSA'S REVENGE

They headed north and soon saw a portal. "Well, here goes nothing," Greg said as they walked through. When they arrived they noticed that their surroundings were beautiful. What they didn't notice was that the dice storm ended when they entered the portal.

"Anyone know where we are?" Izal asked.

"We're in the Celestial Realm. Nowhere else looks like it," Dennis said.

"Do you live here?" Arith asked.

"No, but I've heard of it. I can visit but I'm not allowed to live here. I'm surprised the portal let us out here. Normally mortals aren't allowed here. Someone must've pulled a lot of strings to make this happen," Dennis admitted, still staring at his surroundings.

"That's true. A lot of strings were pulled to make this happen but the real question is why did those strings need to be pulled," a woman's voice said.

"Who are you?" Izal asked.

"I'm the answer to your dilemma. The one who set you on this quest and the one who will end your quest," the voice replied.

"Why did you do this?" Arith asked.

"There were a lot of reasons. You, Izal and Greg were merely in the wrong place at the wrong time or the right place at the right time depending on how you think about it. The real reason this happened is because of Dennis. I have no quarrel with the rest of you and once the trial is over I will ensure that you and Izal are returned to your rightful bodies," the voice promised.

"What about me and the child?" Greg asked, sounding frightened.

"What child?" The voice demanded.

"The one my body is currently carrying. Chaos magic created a mystical pregnancy and until the child's safety is guaranteed I'm not sure my body should be tampered with. The child needs a steady infusion of chaos magic to survive." Greg insisted.

"I see. That does complicate things some. Very well, I will ensure the child is kept safe," the voice promised.

"What do you mean this happened because of me?" Dennis asked.

"Had you not spurned me I would have no reason to hate you. I thought long and hard about what revenge would be best but when my patrons suggested I combine my revenge with your trial I looked for a chance to turn you into something loathsome. I wanted a cockroach but my patron said for it to count as your trial the quest needed the possibility of success. I promised that no-one other than you would be harmed during the quest. I chose a zombie because I didn't think you would respect one and I was right," the voice insisted.

"We told you that your arrogance would cause problems. We should have realized this was your fault," Izal exclaimed, throwing their hands up in disbelief.

"How is this my fault? You don't know that I actually spurned them. All you have is the voice of someone you can't see claiming they did this out of revenge," Dennis complained before turning white. "Greg, I think the child needs chaos magic. I don't feel so good," Dennis said before puking.

"What's happening to him?" The voice asked.

"When the child needs magic it weakens him, drawing off his life force and causing him to become ill until the child receives chaos magic. The child must need a lot of magic because Dennis was given charms by Healer Suzia to prevent vomiting," Arith explained.

"Why isn't Greg doing something about it?" The voice asked.

"Because he still doesn't have the best control of chaos magic and needs time to ensure the magic used won't hurt Dennis or the child." Izal explained.

Finally Greg cast two spells in quick succession. Dennis stopped puking and instead of being white he turned plaid. Everything in a ten foot radius turned colors or patterns. The second spell didn't seem to have done anything yet but everyone knew that didn't mean anything.

"That should be enough for a while. Hopefully I won't need to cast anything else for a while. The child is certainly strong though so we'll see how things play out," Greg admitted.

"This is certainly something I never expected to see. Dennis is pregnant. That's even better than turning him into a cockroach. The girls will never believe this. I'll need to find a way to make sure they can see this." The voice said with glee. There was a moment of silence and the voice spoke again. "Wait here. I will need to inform everyone that there are complications," the voice explained and left them.

They'd been waiting for a while when Arith broke the silence. "Who have you hurt enough to warrant being turned into a Zombie?" Arith asked glaring at Dennis.

"I don't know. They were hiding whcnever they spoke. Their voice sounds familiar but that doesn't tell me much. I have spent a lot of time drinking," Dennis put their hands up to hold off the protests. "In my defense chaos often follows liquor."

"Right. The fact that you enjoy drinking has nothing to do with it, I'm sure." Izal teased.

"That's neither here nor there. I wasn't even given a chance to defend myself," Dennis whined.

"I don't think it matters. You mouthed off to a soothsayer, argued with the leader of my clan, and Arith had to keep the North Wind from obliterating you. If we didn't think it'd be easier to undo the ritual with you I'm pretty sure we'd all leave you to your fate. The worst part is we're in this mess because of you and you've treated us so poorly that we don't really want to defend you. Are you really shocked that someone's punishing you?" Izal asked, staring at Dennis shocked at the lack of self-awareness the former god displayed.

"Does Ressa ring a bell?" The voice from before asked, revealing herself as a woman in white robes.

"Crazy Ressa?" Dennis asked.

The woman glared. "Are you sure you want to go there? I am responsible for your current fate after all." The voice reminded him.

"I think you're going to have to spell it out for him. He's clearly too dumb to put the pieces together on his own." Arith suggested.

"I'm Ressa you idiot. I set this up and I'm responsible for all of it. I told you, you'd rue the day you crossed me," Ressa said, smiling at the dumbfounded look on his face.

"Any chance you want to explain what this idiot did to get on your bad side? I'd like to make sure I don't make the same mistake," Izal said, smiling at Ressa.

"Well, since you asked so nicely. I guess I could tell you. We do have some time to kill before the trial and we can't do anything until then," Ressa admitted before nodding.

"Thank you." Izal said.

"Dennis seemed nice and before I knew it we were dating. He told me he loved me and even offered to make me a minor goddess. Things were going great until I asked for handfasting or a formal courtship. He said I was just a diversion, a bit of fun, but nothing more. I was heartbroken and I vowed to make him regret his callous actions," Ressa admitted, tears streaming down her face as she glared at Dennis.

"I don't understand why it bothers you. We weren't together that long. It was just a few dates. Why'd you have to get attached?" Dennis asked.

"We were together three years, you numbskull. Do you really think my patrons would've let me put you through this if you hadn't actually wronged me? I'm powerful but I'm not powerful enough to bind a deity even a small one against their will. No, you acted so poorly that some of your fellow deities agreed to help me punish you for it," Ressa explained.

"Wow. I knew Dennis was a jerk but that's low even for him. I can't blame you for wanting revenge after that. If it helps I think the North Wind wants to turn him into an eternal chew toy and my clan wants to declare blood feud on him," Izal replied.

"I'm glad to see he hasn't fooled you and I'm sorry you got pulled into this. I just wanted him to pay," Ressa said, giving Arith, Izal and Greg sad looks.

"It's okay. Izal and I are courting now. We might not have met if it weren't for you and I personally am much happier now. I just want to finish my courtship in my own body. I'm sure Izal feels the same," Arith said as Izal nodded their agreement.

Ressa looked at Greg. "What about you? How do you feel about this?" Ressa asked.

"As long as the child is okay I'm willing to accept whatever fate has in store for me. Try to remember that what Dennis did was because of his shortcomings, not yours," Greg said, giving Ressa a smile.

With that said there was nothing left to do but wait for the trial.

Chapter 24
Dennis' Trial

As they were standing there trying to process what had just occurred, they heard a loud bang and saw that a courtroom had sprung up around them. Izal, Arith and Greg had been relegated to the audience and Dennis was in the defendant's seat.

Since they didn't know what happened or what to do about it Izal, Arith and Greg decided to go with it. "All rise as Judge Nakotah enters the courtroom," A voice rang out and everyone jumped up.

A large god walked in. "Judge Nakotah presiding.

Is everyone present and accounted for?" The judge asked.

With a bright flash the courtroom filled up. A demon appeared next to Dennis along with Healer Suzia. "Your honor, may I have a moment to confer with my client. I've just received notice that my client has an unusual medical condition and would like to ensure they're well enough to attend these proceedings at this time. I brought Healer Suzia to assess them. If that's alright with you?" The demon asked.

"As the prosecution and the jury are still missing that should be fine but I would like Healer Suzia to let me know if your client is able to be present for these proceedings," Judge Nakotah said in a tone that made it clear their request is really an order.

"Thank you, your honor," The attorney said.

Judge Nakotah snapped their fingers and a bright light surrounded Dennis, the attorney and Healer Suzia preventing anyone from seeing or hearing them. Fifteen minutes later the attorney came out of concealment. "Thank you for granting us privacy. Healer Suzia has finished her examination and will be out shortly," The attorney said.

Moments later Healer Suzia emerged escorting Dennis to his seat. "Dennis is well enough to attend the trial but I must request that if he weakens he be given an infusion of chaos magic. The child his body is carrying drains him of life energy when its chaos reserves drop too low. The child is innocent of the crimes Dennis has committed. I would like to ask the court to think of that when the time for sentencing arrives," Healer Suzia insisted.

"Thank you Healer. Please feel free to stay for the trial. If you deem it necessary the trial can be paused for medical reasons," Judge Nakotah replied, bowing their head in deference to the determined Healer.

Another bright flash brought the North Wind to the prosecutor's table and an assortment of beings surrounded by glamour into the jury's box. "Now that everyone's present we can begin. Arith, Greg and Izal may be called as witnesses. The court has learned that Dennis is currently pregnant and his health is precarious so we have a Healer on standby. The child is innocent but their existence may be a factor in sentencing. Now we'll start with the prosecution." Judge Nakotah said, banging their gavel.

North stood up. "The defendant Dennis Murphy was a god among men; literally. A minor chaos god but a god nonetheless. He's a loose cannon Your Honor. Despite being warned multiple times to curb his arrogance he hasn't. Even going so far as to insult the leader of the Sunbound Clan while a guest in their home. He broke the Laws of Hospitality and nearly started a Blood Feud. His reckless disregard for rules even led him to questioning if my grandchild would taste good. The fact that he was in a Zombie body when he said it makes it worse. I've had the wind listening to everything he's said since the quest began and bringing me all mentions of his name since he reached godhood. The only good thing anyone's said about him was that he's shown some concern for the child he's currently carrying. Is that enough to pass his trial?" North asked before sitting down.

The demonic attorney stood up. "Your honor my client may not be a sterling example of kindness and decency but who is? If being selfish is enough to have our powers bound many of us would be powerless. It seems a bit harsh to let someone with a known grievance towards my client prosecute them. This started because an ex-lover of Dennis' felt slighted after they broke up. Granted my client was a terrible boyfriend but surely that's not a reason to take away his powers or status as a deity." The attorney asked before returning to their seat.

Only the spells on everyone's chairs kept outbursts from occurring. Unfortunately, it didn't stop Dennis from glaring at his attorney. Finally realizing the magic wouldn't let Dennis speak out of turn, Dennis wrote a note and passed it to his attorney.

I thought you were on my side.

The demon read it before replying on the same scrap of paper.

I am, but that doesn't mean I'm an idiot nor does it mean I can avoid acknowledging when you've screwed up. It's my job to try and prevent you from losing your powers and godhood, not paint you as a paragon of virtue. Besides, when everyone and their cousin knows you're a jerk, trying to pretend otherwise is a waste of time. Now stop distracting me so I can do my job.

North stood. "If Dennis cannot treat other people with respect then it seems unwise to allow him access to powers beyond mortal understanding. We've all heard stories of gods and goddesses who lacked compassion and empathy. I don't think any of us want more deities like that. It's why the trials were invented in the first place. All deities are tested eventually to ensure they are worthy to wield their powers. If Dennis cannot pass the trials then he cannot keep his powers. It's that simple," North insisted.

"So, the guy's not perfect. Do you even know what would happen to him or the child if you did something that drastic. Surely, there must be a more reasonable solution," The attorney questioned.

Judge Nakotah banged their gavel. "Enough! You two keep repeating the same things as if it will change anything. We need to make a decision not bicker like children. If someone has something to add to the conversation, raise their hand. Otherwise we're moving onto sentencing," Judge Nakotah insisted. Scanning the courtroom they were surprised to see Greg's hand up.

Judge Nakotah motioned for Greg to approach the bench. "I have some things to say Your Honor if you'll allow it." Greg said.

"I'll allow it. Walk to the witness stand." Judge Nakotah demanded. "Do you swear to the truth, the whole truth and nothing but the truth?" A court official demanded.

"I swear upon the dirt from my grave that I will tell the truth as I know it with no attempts to lie or prevaricate. If I lie willingly may I return to the dust from whence I rose never to return again," Greg swore glowing as Magic herself acknowledged his vow.

"Good. Now tell the Court what you thought would help them," the court official demanded.

"Dennis is a jerk. I've known him less than a week and I've already found myself wishing we didn't meet. He's rude and arrogant but he offered to show Arith's family the error of their ways within minutes of meeting them. Granted, some of that was because Arith wanted to set him on fire for being a jerk but still. Despite his selfishness he's learned to listen to people he used to view as less than him. It's true that he hasn't changed much but everyone's a work-in-progress and it takes time to change. Dennis' trial shouldn't be considered a failure after less than a week. It should instead be extended. At least give him till the child is born before considering him a complete failure." Greg pleaded.

Dennis' jaw dropped. Whatever he'd been

expecting it wasn't that. Judge Nakotah banged his gavel. "I think we've all heard enough. There are four options for sentencing. Dennis fails his trial and has his powers permanently bound and godhood stripped away never to return. Dennis passes his trial and his powers are returned along with his godhood. Dennis is put on probation with powers and godhood bound. Dennis is put on probation with powers and godhood unbound," Judge Nakotah explained.

The jury walked out of the room still covered in glamour so that none of them could be identified. While they deliberated Dennis turned white again. Healer Suzia was at his side in an instant. "Your Honor Dennis needs an infusion of chaos magic if he's going to be able to remain until sentencing." Healer Suzia explained.

Judge Nakotah nodded. "You have my permission to have magic used in my courtroom." Judge Nakotah motioned for Greg to come over and help.

Greg stood up and said, " I cast Domain of

Empathy." His body began to shimmer with a glittery, orange aura, and he suddenly began an impassioned speech. The aura grew until it filled the whole courtroom. Once he was finished the aura dissipated coating everyone in orange glitter.

"What was that?" Judge Nakotah asked.

"An Area of Effect spell that grants +5 to Empath for anyone in range of the spell including the caster. Not sure why that counts as chaos but it doesn't seem to hurt anyone so I figured it should be fine," Greg said with a shrug.

Judge Nakotah stared at Greg for a moment. "We're in a courtroom waiting for the jurors to return with the sentence for the defendant and it includes glitter so it counts as chaos," Judge Nakotah explained rubbing their temples.

While they were trying to come to grips with what had just happened and brush off the glitter the jury returned. Luckily for Judge Nakotah it didn't look like any of them had been affected by the spell so they didn't have to declare a mistrial. "Jurors, have you made a decision?" Judge Nakotah asked, wanting this to be over. This case was definitely a lot more annoying than the judge expected.

One of the glamoured members of the jury stepped forward. "We have your honor. The defendant Dennis Murphy has failed to complete their trial during the quest but since the trial lasted less than a week we think it's best to place Dennis on probation. The defendant should have their powers bound along with their godhood. Should the defendant manage to pass their trial they will have their powers unbound and their godhood restored. If they fail to pass the trial by the time their probationary period is over they will lose their powers and godhood forever," The jury spokes-being said before sitting down.

"I see. How long does the jury think the probationary period should last?" Judge Nakotah asked.

The jury spokes-being stood up and replied. "Some

of us think until the child is born and others believe it should last until the child reaches adulthood. Both groups feel best about letting you decide that," They said before sitting down once more.

"I see. Thank you for your service. Once I've laid out the sentence you are free to leave. Dennis Murphy this court orders you to begin probation immediately. Your powers will be bound along with your godhood until the child has reached adult status or you've completed your trial whichever happens first. Should you wind up in any further legal trouble for which you have been deemed at fault it will constitute an automatic failure of your trial. Do you understand Mr. Murphy?" Judge Nakotah asked.

"Yes, Your Honor," Dennis replied.

"In that case; court is adjourned," Judge Nakotah said, banging their gavel.

"All rise," The court official said before Judge Nakotah walked out.

CHAPTER 25
AFTERMATH

The courtroom vanished and with it everyone who'd come to the trial except for seven beings. Healer Suzia remained with the four body-swapped beings, the North Wind was there supporting Arith and by extension Izal and an unidentified being wearing a glamour that made them unrecognizable. Arith ran to North and jumped into his arms.

"I've missed you, Papa North," Arith exclaimed.

"Didn't they see him earlier?" Greg asked.

"Doesn't matter. If Arith's happy, I'm happy," Izal

replied.

"You are such a sap," Dennis remarked, sounding snide.

"As I'm the one currently in a Formal Courtship I think it's safe to say you're just jealous," Izal replied smiling as Dennis started fuming.

"Why would I be jealous of you?" Dennis asked.

"Because people like me and I don't have to wonder what their real motives are when they're nice to me. You could also be jealous of my relationship with my family or even just the fact that nobody currently wants me injured, maimed or dead," Izal replied.

Arith laughed. "You don't need to rub Dennis' nose in it. It's much more satisfying when you let them figure it out on their own. Then they can't blame you for pointing it out," Arith teased.

"Dearheart it's time to undo the ritual that brought you together and led you here," North declared.

"Okay but you need to promise the babe will be

safe and that it won't affect my relationship with Izal. I promised Greg that I would be the child's faerie godparent," Arith said, giving their grandfather a serious look.

"Are you sure you're ready for that?" North asked, giving his grandchild a curious look.

"I would not have promised if I didn't mean it. I may not love Izal yet but that will come in time." If Arith had been paying attention they would have heard Izal gasp at hearing they weren't loved and sigh in relief at hearing that Arith believed love would bless their bonding. "The priest who initiated our courtship said our vows of Intention sounded like Bonding Vows and swore we'd be lifemates. The child needs me and being godparents will allow Izal and I time to practice parenting before we have children of our own," Arith explained; as much for Greg, Dennis and Izal as for North.

"In that case I believe it is time for the ritual to come undone. You have my word that the babe will be safe and your Courtship will not be affected negatively," North promised, giving Arith another embrace. "I am so proud of you dearheart. You've grown so much and if Izal is the one that puts this fire in your eyes and flames in your heart I'm sure I'll grow to love them too" North declared, releasing Arith from the hug before pulling Izal into a quick embrace.

The unnamed being stood with Ressa. "Alright, places, everyone! Healer Suzia, North Wind, please stand with us outside the circle," The stranger directed and suddenly everyone could see a ritual circle with a four pointed star inside. None of them knew if the star had been there earlier though.

"Greg, I need you to stand on the Northern point of the star. Dennis, you stand on the southern point. Arith you stand on the Eastern point and Izal you stand on the Western point," Ressa demanded.

Everyone did as she asked and when she gestured for North to stand behind Izal he did. Ressa gestured for Healer Suzia to stand behind Greg, the unknown being stepped up to stand behind Dennis and Ressa moved to stand behind Arith.

"Now that everyone's in place we can move on. None of you speak until I tell you it's over. Any mistakes could result in catastrophic results for one or all of you. Especially since the ritual is complicated by the need to ensure the babe remains safe throughout the ritual," the stranger warned.

"I call the directions, North, East, West, and South. I call Chaos, Fire, Air and Magic. That each of the questors in this circle may know they are represented. I ask a blessing on the child that magic has so graciously gifted us with that they may be protected throughout this ritual and all the ones to come. I ask that Arith and Izal's Courtship not be harmed for Magic herself has blessed their union. I ask that Arith's faerie godchild is kept safe from harm. All these things I ask as I begin this ritual," The stranger said as the circle lit up and each point on the star glowed brighter.

"It is my wish that these four return to their own

bodies. I ask that Greg be returned to the human form we see in front of us and the child remains unharmed. I ask these things because the quest has ended and it is time to put things back to rights," Ressa said, and the points on the star glowed brighter.

"I ask that the earlier ritual be undone. I ask that Arith's faerie godchild remain safe in this time of change. I ask these things because it is time to put this chapter in the past," North said, and the points on the star glowed brighter still.

"I ask that no one is harmed in this ritual. I ask that the health of the babe remains despite the change. I ask that Dennis and Greg be returned to their human forms and that Izal and Arith return to their original bodies. Thank you Chaos, Air, Fire and Magic for your help in this ritual. Thank you South, West, East and North for your help in this ritual. With these words I invoke the changes asked and end the ritual," Healer Suzia said and the points on the star glowed so brightly it blinded them momentarily.

When everyone's vision had recovered they left the circle. "Did it work?" Arith asked in a melodic voice only to smile when looking down at their normal form. "Well, it did for me but we should make sure it worked for everyone before we celebrate," Arith suggested.

"I'm good," Izal intoned happy to be an Ifrit once more.

"It looks like I'm me again and I'm pretty sure I'm not pregnant anymore," Dennis said, realizing that he didn't feel weak or sick.

"I'm me and if things worked out, I think I am pregnant. Healer Suzia would you mind checking?" Greg asked, looking down at his stomach in fear.

"Well, you're definitely still pregnant. Which means we can move onto step two," Healer Suzia said before gesturing for the North Wind to restrain Dennis.

"This is gonna suck but if you're lucky it won't be forever," the stranger said before binding Dennis' powers and godhood. It took a few minutes to set the counter that would make it permanent or undo the spell.

"You have until the child reaches adulthood to pass the trial. Good luck. I didn't think you'd get as close as you have," the stranger admitted.

"How close am I to passing?" Dennis asked.

"Not very, but between the child and Domain of Empathy you're a lot closer than you were. Honestly all of us thought it was hopeless until then. We'll be watching," the stranger promised.

The quest was over. Dennis' fate was uncertain. The child had yet to be born. No-one knew how Greg would parent his miracle baby and of course Izal had yet to fully win over Papa North but that was a different story altogether.